In Plain Sight

Sephira Allen

In Plain Sight

Copyright © 2013 Sephira Allen

sephiraallen.com

Author's Note

From the first shots fired in April 1861 until the last troops laid down their weapons in June 1865, the Civil War was one of the deadliest and most tragic eras in the history of the United States of America. Well over 600,000 soldiers were killed as a result of the hostilities (potentially as many as 750,000 according to new evidence published in 2012), and another nearly half-million were injured. Those figures do not even take into account the civilian losses or the sheer devastation the war left in the various cities that were caught in the crossfire.

Having grown up in Virginia, I was surrounded at all times by the history of the Civil War, and it's a subject that has fascinated me since I was a small child. I spent many days during my childhood hiking the battlefields, digging up minié balls, and uncovering other relics in my aunt and uncle's fields. It's really no wonder that I turned to the subject in this, my first novel.

The events depicted here occurred primarily in November and December 1863. They are loosely set around the tail end of the Bristoe Campaign and Major General George Meade's Army of the Potomac meeting up with General Robert E. Lee's forces at the Second Battle of Rappahannock Station, then continuing several weeks later at the Battle of Mine Run, just before Meade's army made for their Winter camp outside of Brandy Station, Virginia. Also mentioned is the end of the Knoxville Campaign, which took place in December 1863, where General John G. Parke's Army of the Ohio met up with General James Longstreet at the Battle of Bean's Station. Also referenced is the Fall of Petersburg in April 1865, which occurred just days before Lee surrendered to Grant at Appomattox Court House on April 9. Please excuse any inaccuracies and the liberties I've taken with time and distance as it relates to these events.

PROLOGUE

Virginia: May 25, 1843

The screaming stopped.

At first, he wasn't even sure what the difference was. Throughout the day, the sound had been a constant companion and once it was gone, several minutes passed before it dawned on him just what was missing. The screaming had been terrible enough, but he was quite sure the silence was worse. He chewed at his lip, waiting in the warmly lit room where they'd left him, pacing back and forth. The soft woven rug his mother had laid over the hardwood floor muffled the sound of his steps.

"Stay here, out of the way," they'd said. "Don't worry; shouldn't take too long." And with a smile and a kiss, he'd been left alone, with naught but his own thoughts for company. That had been hours ago, but to seven-year-old Matthew James, it seemed an eternity.

His belly rumbled in the empty silence of the room—a not-so-subtle reminder that he'd eaten the lunch and the extra treats they'd left him much too long ago. If only he'd known what *soon* really meant, he might have saved something, any small morsel that would have kept the worst of the pangs away. Shaking his head, he sighed loudly then continued his path back and forth across the room.

The door opened, barely squeaking on its well-oiled hinges. Turning, Matthew watched his father enter and set a tiny, blanket-wrapped bundle carefully into the ornate cradle standing at the far end of the room. He motioned for Matthew to join him, and they looked down at the squalling baby. She was just a little thing, not much to look at—all red-faced and wrinkly—but man, could she holler.

His father reached over, laid a hand on the polished cherrywood frame, and gently rocked the cradle. His face looked haggard. The lines that had been faint only hours earlier - little more than accents to his character, were now deeply etched. His hazel

2

eyes, normally twinkling with joy, echoed the sadness in his heart as he gazed down at his newborn daughter.

Taking a deep breath, he turned those sorrow-filled eyes to Matthew. "Son, it's up to you and me now to take care of her. She's all we have left, and she'll need her big brother more than ever to protect her and keep her safe."

Matthew had been right. The silence was worse, much worse, and as his father's words hit him, Matthew's eyes filled. *Boys don't cry.* He repeated it to himself over and over, biting his lip to keep the tears from spilling over. Even so, it was in vain, and he felt the trail of wetness streak down his face. Ignoring it, he squared his shoulders and looked gravely into his father's eyes. Finally, with only a small quiver in his voice, he replied, "Yes, Papa, I understand. I… I won't let you down."

Lee James hugged his son tight. "You'd be so proud… of both of them." He whispered, looking longingly toward heaven.

Matt barely heard the words as his gaze dropped again to the precious baby in the cradle. But any joy he might have felt at finally having a sister was tempered by the knowledge that it had cost him his beloved mother's life.

CHAPTER ONE

Virginia: November 7, 1863

Rylee James was sitting in her room, mending a tear in her favorite calico skirt. An odious chore to be sure, but one that needed to be done—no matter that she would much rather have been out riding, enjoying the beautiful weather. Though it was late fall and the chill of winter hovered in the air most mornings, they'd had a bit of a warm spell. Grateful for the break in the weather, she'd flung her windows wide open to take advantage of the fresh air and even now gazed longingly at the clear blue skies.

Sighing heavily, Rylee turned back to the skirt and focused on pulling the needle in and out of the fabric. The stitches were less than neat, but given her distracted nature, it was probably the best that could be expected. Besides, they would hold well enough in the end, and that was all that really mattered.

Her mind drifted again, and she sat, daydreaming in the warm glow of the sun, until the sound of hoofbeats pounding on the hard-packed dirt road brought her swiftly back to her room. "Damn!" she cried, as the needle bit into the soft flesh of her palm. Hand still stinging, she wiped at the crimson drop that was forming, as she heard booted feet run up the front porch steps.

"Ry… You in there?" her brother yelled as he swung open the front door.

Taking care not to get blood on the skirt, Rylee set her sewing aside then hurried out of her room and down the stairs toward the porch, almost running her brother down as he came through the doorway. "Matthew James, what in the world is wrong with you?"

She hadn't seen him in months, and it was a shock to see how thin and hard he'd become. His normally sparkling green eyes looked tired, and she wrapped her arms around him in welcome, wishing that she would never have to let go again.

"There's not much time, Ry." He stepped back from her embrace. "The Union troops aren't very far behind us. We couldn't hold the river, and we have to fall back. Can't stay, but I'll be back in a few days to check on you."

"Do you really think they will come through this way?" She tried to conceal the slight note of fear in her voice. "It's not like we have anything left to give them, and now that Pa is gone…" Her voice trailed off as fresh grief threatened to overwhelm her. Even though it had been over a year, she still missed her pa something fierce. Just thinking of him was enough to make her heart hurt.

Matt grabbed her arm. "Don't let them know that Pa is gone. Make up whatever excuse you need to, but if they find out you're here alone, there will be nothing but trouble."

Ry rolled her eyes at him. "I can take care of myself, you know. Besides, I'm not completely alone. Katie and Samuel are still here with me."

"I do know," he said. "I taught you myself." The prideful grin sneaked across his face, but he quickly sobered. "It wouldn't be enough for some of these men, and I don't want to see my baby sister getting hurt."

"Don't you worry about us. We'll be fine. Besides, you're the one I should be worried about. Every day, I'm terrified that someone is going to bring word to me that you're dead." Her eyes were full of unshed tears, and she turned away quickly before he could see them fall. The last few years had taken a toll on them all, especially since the death of their father. "I really don't know how I'd go on if you were gone too," she whispered, her voice thick with emotion.

They had been so proud when Matt had been accepted to West Point, and he'd graduated with honors as well. Little had they known that war was right around the corner. Taking a deep breath, Rylee brushed away the tears then turned back to face her brother.

Matt moved to her side and put his arms around her shoulders, resting his head against hers for a moment. There were no words he could say, but the contact was enough for now. Giving her arm a final squeeze, he sighed and let her go, turning reluctantly toward the door. "I've got to head back. Keep close to the house and lock everything up tight tonight."

Ry ran after him and threw her arms around him again. Desperately, she held on, no longer caring if he saw that tears that streamed down her face. "Be safe," she whispered before planting a kiss on his brow.

"You too." He gently wiped away her tears. Then he mounted up and rode off, his horse kicking up the dirt as he raced back down the lane.

She stood watching until he was out of sight, then closed the door and walked slowly to the kitchen to warn her housekeeper of the possible incursion. Though the sun was still shining, there was a chill in her heart that had nothing to do with the weather.

"Katie… we need to get ready. It's going to be a long night."

The late afternoon sun blazed low in the sky, its orange and red hued beams almost even with the horizon, when the first Union troops began passing through. At first, they kept to the fields farther out, and Ry sincerely hoped they stayed there, as far away from the house as possible. Wishful thinking on her part, but it was all she had to go on, so she clung to it. She was helping Katie with dinner when reality finally came crashing in. The loud banging on the front door startled them both, and immediately Ry's temper flared. Her head jerked toward the sound, and she fought the urge to grab her rifle, wanting nothing more than to give whoever it was a huge piece of her mind. Only Katie's calming hand on her arm brought her up short.

"Miss Rylee, you need to go hide now," Katie murmured as she started walking toward the door, another round of loud knocks beckoning. "Samuel and I will take care of this. Go on now… and don't let them see you."

"Yes, Katie, I'm going. Please be careful!"

Reluctantly, Ry moved toward the back staircase and up to her father's room. When she was just a little girl, she'd discovered a small storage area hidden in one of the walls. While the entrance itself was fairly low to the ground, it was much larger on the inside and had been the perfect place for her to play her silly adventure games. This would be completely different, of course, but with little in the way of options, it was the best thing for her to do.

Upon entering the room, Ry took a quick peek out the window. Inhaling sharply, her breath caught in her chest and she grasped onto the frame, willing the darkness that hovered at the edges of her vision to go away. She had never been prone to fainting spells— she would have rather died before showing any such weakness around her brother, but there was always a first time for everything. Matt had warned her that the

Union soldiers were coming, but knowing and seeing were two completely different things.

Already, there were several dozen tents set up in the field closest to the house, interspersed with figures in blue. Now that the sun was setting in earnest, campfires had been lit here and there, a stark contrast to the twilight that was quickly fading into the true darkness of night. Faced with reality, the brave words Ry had used to comfort her brother earlier seemed hollow and empty. Not wanting to tempt fate any longer, she moved to conceal herself, taking care to ensure the entrance was hidden from anyone who might dare to look.

Her father's room was at the front of the house and featured several large floor-to-ceiling windows which opened onto a narrow balcony, where, in happier times, she and her father had often sat at night to talk or look at the stars. So now, even from within her hiding place, Ry could hear most of what was going on in the front hall. Listening intently, she heard Katie open the door, and had to quickly cover her mouth with her hand to keep from laughing out loud when she heard Katie's polite and respectful, "How may I help you gentlemen?" It was as though Katie had found nothing more than a lost traveler or two standing on the porch, or a neighbor who had ridden over to ask for some much-needed assistance, rather than a whole legion of Union soldiers hell-bent on making their lives as miserable as possible.

The reply, when it came however, was enough to wipe the smile off of Rylee's face. Though also polite, it held an underlying tone of arrogance. Here was a man who was used to giving orders and having them obeyed instantly. No doubt he would do whatever he wanted, whether they liked it or not. "Captain Elijah Webb, ma'am, at your service. Please inform the master of the house that we would like to speak with him immediately. We will be camping here tonight, and we have orders to gather any supplies as needed."

Katie, unflappable as ever, simply said, "Mister James is not in residence at the moment, just my husband and myself. We will do our best to comply with your orders, though truthfully, we've not much else left to give."

There was a brief pause, and Ry strained to hear the officer's reply. "Well… you are free now, you know, since the president's decree, I mean." He said it awkwardly, as if not quite sure how to approach the subject, and Ry smiled at his discomfort. "If you'd like, we can help you get safe passage up to the north when we go."

"Thank you for your concern, but you misunderstand me," Katie said. "This is our home, and we have no intention of going anywhere. Mister James hasn't owned slaves here in years. He didn't need any sort of proclamation to do what was right for his people. Samuel and I stay on because we want to. This is where our family is."

"I see." Without another word on the subject, the officer addressed his own men, "Cam, make sure they are finished setting up and that everyone is fed. I don't want any nonsense tonight. We'll want to get started early in the morning; the major wants us back at the main encampment as soon as possible. If you need me, I'll be in here tonight, inventorying the supplies that we will take with us." Without waiting for a reply, Ry heard him step fully into the house and close the door. The sound of his boots echoing loudly through the house as he followed Katie down the hall.

The unexpected warmth they'd enjoyed during the day had long since faded, and true to the season, the coming of night brought with it much colder temperatures. Still, the skies were clear, and the smallest sounds carried far on the chilling breeze. Ry could hear the men outside settling down for the night, and though she chafed at having to hide like a scared child, she knew she didn't have much of a choice. She and Katie had stocked the room earlier with a bit of food and water, so with nothing much left to do, Ry ate a small meal, then despite it all, started to doze.

She awoke a short while later at the sound of footsteps in her father's room, each step as loud as a hammer to a nail. Standing carefully, she peeked through a small crack in the wall and was startled to see the Union officer. It made sense, of course. Given the option between sleeping on the cold, hard ground or a nice warm bed, the bed was the obvious choice. For some reason, it just hadn't occurred to her that he would violate the sanctity of her father's room.

Ry fought to control her anger and continued to watch as the soldier walked around the room. It had changed little since her father's death. She'd kept it as a shrine of sorts to the man whose passing had left such a gaping void in their lives, it was still sometimes hard to believe that he was gone. Though it was no longer used, she and Katie still took turns cleaning and dusting, occasionally putting fresh flowers on the tables. Even now, if she pressed her face into his pillow, Ry could sometimes catch his scent. Her father may have no longer been present in the flesh, but it was no reason not to honor his spirit. She was thankful

16

now that they hadn't changed too much, and she prayed there was nothing that would give away the fact that no one had been using the room for quite some time.

If they'd met under different circumstances, Ry was sure she might have actually been impressed with Captain Webb. Really, what woman doesn't find a tall, well-built man attractive? He appeared to be about the same age as her brother, but where Matt was fair like their mother, Elijah Webb was dark as the night sky. She assumed that his eyes would match his raven hair, but when he turned, she saw they were a piercing blue—a color so deep that any woman would be more than happy to sink into their depths.

She shook her head at the thought then grimaced. Too bad he was currently commandeering her house, intent on stealing anything not nailed down. Facts that made her less inclined to swoon at his feet. "I'd much rather have him groveling or better yet, my knife in his ribs," she whispered viciously.

Angry, she started to pace then stopped herself, remembering all too well that the old floorboards were likely to creak with every step. Shaking off her nervous energy, she sighed. To be fair, Captain Webb had thus far treated Katie and Samuel well, and thankfully, he didn't seem intent on trashing the place out of spite. But she knew too, that when he moved on, he would be taking most of what little she had left. Even worse, he would be going off to kill men like her brother—good men, who were just unlucky enough to get stuck on the wrong side of this stupid war.

Fed up with it all, she turned away. Eyeing the small cot, she sighed again, silently lamenting that she hadn't brought in an extra blanket for padding. As a bed, the cot would do in a pinch, but it was seriously lacking in comfort and definitely not something that anyone would want to sleep on for the long term. Climbing in, she settled as best she could, but sleep eluded her, and as the hours passed, she found herself wide-awake, staring uselessly at the wall.

~*~

The sound of more footsteps in the hallway had her back out of bed in an instant, and she watched in silence as another officer stepped into the room.

"Captain Webb, everything is set," he said. "We will be ready to load up the supplies at first light and move out. Also, a messenger arrived. Seems we managed to catch some of those bastards that were running from the river. Should be some fun times when we get back to camp." The words were punctuated by a vicious grin, and the thinly disguised glee sent shivers down Ry's back. Her gut twisted sharply, and she fought the urge to vomit up the meager dinner she'd eaten earlier in the evening.

"Thank you for delivering the message. Dismissed." Eli barely acknowledged the man as he left, too intently focused on reading the rest of the missive in his hands. "Damn, Matthew, looks like your luck finally ran out," he said after a few moments, shaking his head.

Still struggling with her disgust, at first Ry thought Eli was speaking to her. He was facing the wall concealing her, and they were very nearly eye to eye. Too afraid to move for fear he might notice the shifting light, she stood there stock-still. In her mind, she visualized her father's room, and it took only a moment to realize the captain was looking at the family portrait hanging on the wall. She never stopped to wonder how he knew her brother, for just then, his words came back to her in a rush.

Oh God... No!

With despair filling her heart, it took all she had not to cry out, but even so, Ry couldn't keep the tears from streaking down her cheeks. Matthew had used up precious time to come home and give her warning, leaving him none left with which to escape. "You fool!" she cried silently. There was absolutely no doubt in her mind he'd been taken because of her. She wanted to scream at the unfairness of it all, and when Eli finally turned away from the wall, she stumbled back to her bed and sobbed softly into her pillow.

Never one to wallow in self-pity for long, though, her despair quickly turned to anger. Drying her tears, her mind raced ahead, fueled by the rage that was slowly building inside the spaces so recently hollowed out by her grief. The glimmer of an idea hovered at the edge of reason, and as she pulled at each shimmering thread, a plan began to take shape. Not only could she help her brother, but she would make these Union pigs wish they'd never stepped foot on her property.

For a brief moment, she considered coming right out and stabbing the bastard sleeping in her father's bed. She caught herself, but just barely. The knife was in her hand when common sense finally kicked in. Realizing, as she was preparing to open the hidden door, that being surrounded by a hundred or so of Eli's fellow soldiers probably wasn't the best time to do such a thing—at least not if she wanted to live to tell the tale. So as with any good bit of revenge, Rylee would bide her time and wait for the right moment, then serve up the coldest damn dish they'd ever tasted.

Shifting carefully to the bed, she lay back down and pulled her blankets up tight around her shoulders. Willing herself to be calm, she drifted off to sleep as exhaustion finally took hold. Dreaming of what was to come, she waited out the rest of the night safely hidden, not daring to come out until Katie knocked to let her know that all the troops were long gone from the area.

CHAPTER TWO

Virginia: November 8, 1863

Ry sat in front of the mirror for a long time. Sunken into her overly pale face, her emerald eyes were dull and shadowed, as the sparkling cheval glass reflected back, in minute detail, all the pain and sorrow she was carrying deep within her heart. Sighing, she examined the lock of hair twisted loosely between her fingers. It too seemed limp and lifeless in the morning sunlight. Truth be told, she wasn't much for vanity. It was hard to be vain growing up in a house with mostly men, but God, she loved her hair. Loved the way it curled to profusion in soft auburn waves that glinted like fire in the sunlight. Loved the way it trailed out behind her in the warm summer breezes when she galloped across the fields. Without it, she would not be herself, which of course was the point, but even so, the moment weighed heavy.

"It will grow back, you ninny!" she whispered to her reflection, even as she continued to mourn its loss. Finally, recognizing she was only stalling the inevitable—it absolutely had to be done if she was ever going to make this work—she gathered her resolve.

Katie stood just behind her, razor-sharp shears in hand, and for a moment, her brown eyes met Ry's in the mirror, asking without words, "Are you sure?"

Ry nodded briefly in answer then stilled as Katie raised the shears to her hair. But regardless of her determination to follow through, the glint of unshed tears remained as the long auburn tresses hit the floor.

Despite it all, the close-cropped style actually suited her. She ran her fingers through it a few times before settling on a slightly messy look rather than one that was more clean-cut. Once her hair was gone, the rest was easier in a way. She'd been wearing Matt's old cast-offs for years when they'd gone out riding, so there were plenty of clothes to choose from as she dressed and packed up the few things she would need to get her through the next few weeks. Making sure her breasts were well-bound, she finished buttoning up her shirt then took a last look around to make sure she wasn't forgetting anything.

Not even out the door, yet already she wanted to lie down and rest for a bit. The grief and worry threatened to take over, if only she would give them free reign. Instead, she kept moving. If she stopped to think or feel, she would lose her mind. Nearly ready, she grabbed her father's medical bag from the closet and double-checked the supplies. They normally kept it fully stocked for emergencies, but it never hurt to make sure, especially since her skills and that bag were at the heart of her plan. Without it, she would not get far.

Katie and Samuel had tried to talk her out of it, of course, protesting and threatening, until their voices were hoarse with it all. In truth, their advice was sound as always, and in some small way, Ry desperately wanted to give in to them. In the end, though, she had no choice. Matt was the only family she had left. As much as she had loved her father, he'd been rather distant after her mother's death. Many a time in their childhood, Matt had wistfully described their father with twinkling eyes and a sunny smile for all, the echoes of his booming laughter frequently ringing from the rafters.

It was a direct contrast to the somber, sad-eyed man she'd known all her life. Not that anyone could really blame him. He'd loved their mother more than anything, and when she died giving birth to Ry, it was as though a light had gone out. Unfortunately for them all, Lee James had never really recovered. Oh, he'd still provided for them. As a doctor, his services were always needed, and he had been well-respected in the community. To be sure as well, Ry and her brother had never wanted for anything, but her care and general upbringing had largely fallen to Katie and then later, once she could walk, to Matt. Though he never complained about it—well… not too much, anyway— she had been a trial to him, following him everywhere for years. She might have gotten her medical skills from her father, but almost everything else she knew about how to survive in life, she'd learned from her brother. It was time to use those skills to get him back.

"You absolutely sure you want to do this?" Katie asked her again, for what seemed like the hundredth time.

"I have to, and you know it." Her voice was resolute, taking care to hide any trace of the lingering doubts that swirled inside. If Katie knew she was wavering, she would keep needling until Ry broke, and Ry couldn't afford for that to happen, not with Matt's life hanging in the balance. "Besides, if I don't do it, who will?"

For all her determination, she was near to tears again as Katie hugged her tight. "You just be careful, girl. Don't need to lose both of you... you hear! Matt wouldn't want you to get yourself killed for him."

"Maybe not, but he would do the same for me. So I can't do any less for him." She gave Katie's hand one last squeeze. "Don't you worry. I'll be back before you know it."

"Mm-hmm, you'd better be," Katie said, shaking her head.

Samuel stood at Katie's side as always, and they watched with concern as Ry grabbed her gear. Waving to them both, she headed off, afraid that if she waited much longer, she would lose her nerve.

CHAPTER THREE

Virginia: November 9, 1863

Eli's quarter horse raced through the field as if demons straight from the bowels hell were chasing him down. Though, considering all he had seen in the last twenty-four hours, it was more likely the demons were in front of him rather than behind him. What a difference a day made. Relentless rain had come on the heels of the brief warm spell they'd all enjoyed—unending sheets of it. Eli was forever thankful that it hadn't turned to ice, but nonetheless, coupled with the cold, it made for miserable travel. He'd had just enough time to backtrack to the battlefield before it started pouring down.

It had finally let up, but now he was mud-spattered and tired. Fervently, he wished he was home in his own bed—hell, any bed—rather than out in this mess. At this point, even the house he had stayed in two nights ago would have been preferable, though he wasn't sure the owners would feel the same way once they learned he'd had his troops there. Couldn't be helped, really. The soldiers needed food and a place to stay, and the landowners had to do their part, no matter what side of the fence they might be on.

As if any of them had much of a choice these days. He was so sick of this war, and both sides be damned—if he thought he could walk away and not be shot for it, he would have done it a long time ago.

Clearly, some of my men are feeling the same way.

His eyes narrowed at the thought. Whereas Eli only wanted to find a nice quiet hidey-hole in which to ride out the rest of the war, apparently some of his men were taking out their frustrations in more destructive ways. He ran his hands over his face, trying to scrub away the horror.

"Monsters… that's what they are!" His little side trip back to the battlefield had shown him the evidence of that quite plainly. Even now, the memory of the mutilated bodies was almost more than he could handle, and he fought the bile that rose hotly in his throat. He'd really hoped Cam had been mistaken, but the coded message had been straight to the point, and now he was going to have to figure out exactly who was involved and how to make them stop before it happened again. Not only that, but given the prisoners they'd captured in this latest battle, he needed to get back to camp as quickly as possible to make sure someone didn't decide to have a bit more *fun* with their captives. Exasperated, he growled, urging his horse to pick up the pace.

The shots came out of nowhere, cracking loudly in the silence that otherwise surrounded him. If he'd not been lost in thought, the shooters would have never caught him off guard, but the lack of sleep on top of everything else had him spread a bit thin.

"Son of a bitch!" he yelped as the searing pain burned across his left bicep. He was damn lucky that whoever it was had really bad aim. "Good way to get yourself killed," he muttered to himself as he tried to get his bearings and determine exactly who was shooting at him.

The good news, if there was such a thing, was that there were only three of them, or at least, only three that he could see. The bad news—and there was always bad news—was that they looked like deserters, and they were likely hell-bent on making sure that anyone who saw them deserting wouldn't live to tell about it. Unfortunately for Eli, the open field he was crossing offered little in the way of shelter. His only option was to keep riding and hope like hell that he could make it to the wooded area that marked the edge of the farmstead he was riding through.

For a brief moment, he seriously considered calling out to the men. After all, why would a Union soldier care if a bunch of Confederates wanted to head for the hills—just that many less to fight tomorrow. Hell, he would be perfectly happy if every one of them made a run for it. Then they could all just go home and do what they could to put this godforsaken war far behind them.

Sadly, the soldiers in front of him didn't look as though they were in the mood to listen to reason. Of course, if they'd been anywhere near the receiving end of what he'd seen evidence of the night before, he couldn't blame them for feeling that way, either. Shooting would be too kind for the men who'd committed those atrocities. With any luck, Eli would still be alive to make sure those responsible paid horribly for it. As the hoofbeats drew ever closer to him, though, he was starting to wonder if maybe his own luck was running out.

While they had stopped shooting at him, it was still clear they were intent on riding him down. It was just as likely they were saving up their ammunition for when they were a bit more up close and personal. He really did not want to kill them, but if it came down to keeping himself alive, he wasn't going to have much of a choice. Kneeing his horse, he leaned low in the saddle and rode like the wind, praying to any God that would listen for some kind of miracle.

~*~

The rain had been unexpected, and Ry spent a good portion of the day sheltered as best she could under a large tree. Nearly dry, she was eating a bit of lunch, still trying to figure out exactly how to infiltrate the Union camp, when she heard the shots. Creeping carefully to the edge of the woods, she watched three ragged-looking soldiers chasing down a lone rider. While he clearly had the better horse, the desperation of the three soldiers gave them an almost unholy determination and purpose. It gave her pause to know how close she'd been to the deserters. Even worse, she hadn't even known it. It would have not ended well if they'd found her first, and she shivered at the thought. Though she wasn't really affiliated with either side, she didn't think these men would have cared much. She needed to be more careful if she expected to make it through the next few weeks.

Not wanting to risk having all of her careful planning go to waste, Ry started moving back into the woods. Though not a dense forest by any means, the trees werc plentiful enough, and it would be easy to find a place to conceal herself—at least long enough for the danger to pass. As she took a last look before turning away, something about the Union soldier caught her attention. They were all still a fair distance out, but as he drew closer, she realized that he looked very familiar. Knowing that she'd not been in the presence of very many Union soldiers in her life, it hit her suddenly that there was really only one person it could be.

"Well, well. Must be my lucky day," she said with a chuckle.

Working to contain her glee, Ry moved quickly through the trees, circling a bit farther to the south of the riders. Not only so they wouldn't run her down when they hit the tree line, but also so that she would be in a better position to take action when the time came. Settling herself, she carefully aimed her rifle and took the first shot. She briefly lamented the loss of the horse, but she wasn't looking to kill anyone if she could possibly avoid it.

Her father's Henry rifle was one of her most prized possessions, and with it, she had no trouble hitting her target. The horse went down with a loud squeal, throwing its rider hard into the icy mud. The other two Confederate deserters pulled up, gazing warily into the woods, trying desperately to determine whether they were riding into an ambush. As the silence stretched on, prudence eventually won out. Moving quickly, eyes still on the trees, they grabbed their fallen companion and rode off in the opposite direction.

For his part, Eli never even hesitated. Whereas the shot from the woods had stopped the others immediately in their tracks, he realized right away a simple truth—if whomever was shooting had wanted him dead, they would have shot him first. Judging the trajectory, he had a fairly good idea of just where the shooter was hiding, and he'd been a much closer target for sure. So rather than wait around to see what the deserters were going to do about it, he kept going. Grateful for the chance to get to the safety of the trees, he wasn't going to waste it. Maybe his luck was holding out after all.

Once he hit the woods, though, he slowed. It was colder there, darker, as the taller trees blocked what little light there was from the overcast sky. He'd been riding hard even before his new *friends* had shown up, and he knew his poor horse was almost blown. As soon as he was sure no one else was ready to gun him down, he would walk for a bit. He couldn't afford to stop entirely, especially since he was so close to his destination. But to his horse, shedding the six foot three, nearly two-hundred-pound man from his back would help immensely.

As his eyes adjusted to the darkness, he scanned the area for any signs of the lone shooter or anything at all that might indicate there was a larger force of men camping nearby. His own men were headquartered on the other side of the woods at the main encampment, but that didn't mean there might not be other forces moving through. He'd just about decided he was the only one still around, when he came upon a small camp. From the gear hastily stowed in some bushes and the dirt-covered fire that was still emitting lazy tendrils of smoke, odds were in his favor that this was the shooter's site.

"Maybe a bit of a break would do us some good," he said, looking down at his horse. As he dismounted, he could almost hear Ol' Red sigh in relief. "Poor boy." Eli gave him a quick scratch behind the ears. "I promise to give you a good rub down and extra oats when we get back." Taking the time to stir up the embers for some warmth, he sat on the ground, his back up against the nearest tree to wait.

Ry noticed the smoke as she walked back toward her camp. In the fresh clean air of the woods, the acrid smell was an unwelcome intrusion. True, she had been in a rush earlier when she'd left, but Matt had trained her well over the years. She knew the disaster that lurked with an uncovered fire. Even with the rain, it would only take one tiny spark for the crisp fall foliage covering the ground to go up in a fiery blaze, trapping her and anything else foolish enough to get caught in its destructive path. The leaves that were perfect tinder for an out of control fire, were also perfectly noisy when crunched underfoot. So, with a bit more caution, she moved slowly through the trees, choosing her path with the utmost care to avoid detection. Still, she nearly laughed out loud when she saw how things were falling into place for her. It was almost too easy.

Not wanting to startle the captain unnecessarily, she made a conscious effort to be more conspicuous as she walked. She definitely did not want him to think she was trying to sneak up on the camp, or worse, for him to shoot first and ask questions later. Getting shot would not fit in well with her plans to rescue Matt, but other than that, him being there was the answer to her prayers.

Peering through the brush, Ry saw the lone Union soldier dozing by the fire. Despite her efforts to be somewhat noisier, if she'd really wanted to, she could have probably walked right up to him and he would have never known until it was too late. It was clear that his exhaustion was getting the better of him. She stopped for a moment, searching the ground for the perfect stick, then with careful precision, stepped on it with enough force that the resounding crack echoed loudly in the otherwise silent air. She stopped again and watched the captain startle from sleep. He was halfway between dreams and waking, and it was only at the last minute that his mind registered the sound for what it was. She could see that he was fighting to control his urge to panic, as he scrambled to clear his head.

"Don't be alarmed. Just wanted to thank you for your timely intervention." Eli called out, hoping like hell that he had read the situation correctly and wasn't about to get shot.

Well, Ry, this is the moment of truth.

Up to now, everything she'd done had been easy, or at least relatively easy, but if she couldn't convince this man of who she was, all would be lost right here and now. Shaking inside, she briefly considered abandoning her plan and making a run for it while there was still time. "Get a hold of yourself, Ry. Matt's counting on you," she whispered. Taking a deep breath to settle her nerves, she readied herself for the challenge.

"Well, you know… three against one just didn't seem fair," she said conversationally as she walked into the clearing, taking care to deepen her voice just a bit.

While under normal circumstances, no one would ever mistake her for a man, she'd never had any sort of dainty, girly voice, and for once, she was mightily glad of that fact. It made carrying out her plan a whole lot easier. Still, she could hear the tremor in her voice and struggled desperately to control it.

"I'm rather pleased you felt that way," Eli responded. Rising from his position on the ground, he reached out a hand and introduced himself. "Captain Elijah Webb, United States Army."

She took his hand and shook it firmly, thankful again that she'd grown up in a house full of men. "Doctor James Rylee, at your service," she said, echoing the words he'd used to Katie back at the house. "But most people just call me Ry."

She'd thought carefully about what name to use, settling eventually on the reverse of her own, rather than risking the danger of making one up out of whole cloth. She'd been much too afraid that under pressure, she would forget the new one. It would only take once or twice of not responding when called before someone would get suspicious. Using her own had been out of the question as well. There were simply too many people in the area that knew her family, her father in particular, and she didn't think it would be prudent for fear that someone would recognize it. Thankfully, only her brother and Katie ever called her Ry, so though it was familiar to her, it was still safe enough to use. Thoughts drifting again, she realized belatedly that Eli was still talking to her, so she brought her attention back to him.

"…have to ask, though, why in the world would you be traveling through here alone?" he was asking. "Obviously, you seem capable of taking care of yourself, but still, things aren't very safe here right now."

"I'm a doctor. When I'm called on for help, I go." She shrugged, as though traveling through a war-torn area was nothing more than a simple Sunday stroll. "I'm fairly good at staying out of the way when necessary. Speaking of which, I should look at your arm. It's bleeding." Nodding at his arm, she motioned him closer.

Eli looked down at his arm, surprised at the amount of blood that had stained his sleeve. After the initial sting of pain, it had completely slipped his mind, and he started to wave her off, "It's just a scratch, really. Nothing to trouble yourself about."

Ry crossed over to where her gear was stowed. "Nonsense! If you don't at least clean it, it could fester and then something simple ends up with your arm getting cut off." She put a small pot on the fire and poured some water into it. "Now take off your shirt and let me have a look."

Being threatened with losing an arm over something so stupid, Eli quickly reconsidered. "Yes, sir!" he said, with a mocking half salute. He definitely could not afford to lose an arm, especially over a bunch of rotten deserters. So without further arguments, he unbuttoned his shirt and set it to the side.

Ry felt a thrill of excitement run through her. In truth, it was a double victory, not only because he'd allowed her to treat the wound, but he had called her "sir." So far, she was passing the test with flying colors. Of course, it was probably a good thing that her

44

mind was focused on impressing him with her skills, because when she turned to take a look at his arm, her tongue turned to ashes in her mouth. The words "well built," which her mind had assigned to him not more than two days ago, were truly just an understatement. Evil bastard or not, he was very nearly perfect. She sighed, her fingers itching to glide their way over the smooth skin of his chest.

Even though he was sweaty and mud-covered, swooning at his feet would be easy. How could any woman resist those rippling muscles? Shaking her head, she pinched herself hard, a sharp reminder that this was no time for silly daydreams. Cautioning herself, she brought her mind back to the task at hand and the fact that this man was the key to getting her brother back safely.

"Hold on… this might sting a bit," she said, laughing at his brief yelp of pain as she cleaned the wound. "Going to need a couple of stitches too, I think. It's not deep, but it will bleed a lot if I leave it open."

He nodded in agreement. "You're the expert; just do what you need to do."

For Eli, the experience was just a bit disconcerting. He had little doubt that Ry was competent at treating injuries, but for a moment, he would have sworn that the man treating him was actually a woman—except no woman he had ever met would be caught dead looking like that. He knew that size didn't necessarily have anything to do with a man's strength or abilities, but as far as he could tell, it was a good thing this one had gone into medicine. At around five foot ten, he wasn't the shortest man Eli had ever seen, but he was rather on the skinny side with a somewhat delicate build. Still, they could always use another good doctor at camp, especially if he got back and found that anyone else had been mistreating the prisoners.

After mulling it over in his mind, the decision came fairly easily to him. "So I was wondering... how would you feel about coming back to camp with me for a while? Wouldn't have to necessarily join up...

46

well, unless you wanted to." He noted the flare of interest in Ry's eyes. "But I'm sure that there will be those who could use some extra medical attention, especially after these last few days. We have our own medical staff of course, but they can always use a hand at times like these."

Thoughts of the last couple of days and the possibility that her brother was likely one of the wounded sent shivers down Ry's back, and her eyes narrowed briefly in suppressed rage.

Eli, who had been watching intently, was startled by the change that came over her. The look was gone quickly, though, replaced by the more easygoing one she'd been wearing before, and after a few moments, he was sure he must have imagined it.

"Um... sure," she finally nodded, trying hard to keep her emotions in check. "I was heading up that way anyways to see if there was anything I could do to help." She finished tying up the bandage and patted his shoulder "All done here. We can head out whenever you're ready."

Rested or not, Eli walked beside his horse for the remainder of the journey. Ry was on foot, and while Ol' Red normally could have carried them both, at least for short distances, the way Eli had been mistreating the poor brute the last couple of days had him in no such shape. They'd simply rearranged his packs to include Ry's gear then set out toward the east, reaching the encampment a few hours later.

"Didn't realize that there were so many troops out this way," Ry said, staring in awe. The force that Eli had brought to her house was nothing compared to the vast sea of blue that stretched out in front of her.

"Well, there are several companies here at the moment. Mostly just to secure the area and wait for injuries to heal up a bit. When everything is settled, they'll move on to a more permanent winter camp. If you'll follow me, my men are quartered over this way. Should be a spare bunk you can use, and it's close enough to where you'll likely be doing most of your work."

"Mmmm." She nodded, distractedly trailing after him.

It was hard knowing that Matt was so close. All she really wanted to do was run to him, but given the circumstances, she prudently restrained herself. Still, her eyes took in everything as they walked further into the camp.

CHAPTER FOUR

Virginia: November 10, 1863

Matt was dreaming of home—the large three-story Greek colonial, with its graceful columns gleaming in the sunlight. Ry and Katie were standing on the wide front porch, wishing him well as he rode off to join his men. The sights and smells were so strong and vivid in his memory, he was quite sure that if he just reached out his hand he could touch them. His sister's lilting voice echoed in his head, almost as though she was still right there with him.

Startled by shouting outside his window, Matt roused himself from sleep, finding—much to his chagrin—that he was still within the cold, damp confines of his cell. Shaking his head, he sighed and leaned back up against the wall, clutching the thin wool blanket to his chest. It wasn't much, but he would take what he could get against the November chill. The wound just below his rib cage was still painful, and every movement sent white-hot spikes through his skull. But he supposed, since they'd bothered to patch him up, he was going to live.

"Well, at least until they decide my life no longer serves a purpose," he mused.

Helpless to prevent it, Matt had seen the way some of these soldiers had treated others in his command. It sickened him still, that any human being could be so depraved. Even now, he worried they were just waiting for him to get well enough so they could do the same to him. Making him feel safe, only to rip his world away completely. More likely than not, he'd go mad in there first just thinking about it.

"We keep the prisoners in here," Eli said, drawing Ry's attention to a small ramshackle-looking building to his right. Though the top level was mostly open to the elements, the lower floor was sturdy enough, and bars had been added haphazardly to the windows to keep the prisoners in. "To be sure, it's not much to look at from the outside, but it is secure."

Ry noted immediately the advantages of the building—foremost being that it was smack in the middle of the encampment. Even if someone managed to escape their cell, they would still have to go through nearly the entire camp in order to get away. No small feat, given the company they were keeping. She sighed, silently contemplating what it would take to get her brother out of such a place.

The day had been a difficult one already. She'd risen early, hoping to get a start on the task at hand, only to find Eli up and ready to give her a full tour of the facilities. Dreading the idea of spending any more time in his presence than necessary, but seeing no plausible way to decline, she accepted the invitation.

"Might as well know what I'm up against," she mused, resigning herself to being in his company for the day.

There were some positives, though. At least she was bunking close to the prison building, and as there were several injured prisoners, she had been assigned to help. It gave her a huge advantage to be able to come and go in the area rather than having to sneak around. Of course, she still needed to get inside and actually assess her brother's injuries. In just the little time she had been here, she'd already heard rumors about how they'd been treating some of those that had been captured. She was praying that her brother had been spared such horrors.

Admittedly, it was hard to reconcile the rumors with the man she knew Eli to be. Despite her own very valid reasons for disliking him—though she had only been around him for a couple of days—he truly didn't seem the type to put up with such things, especially from men under his own command. When she and Eli had left her camp yesterday, he'd led them straight to the compound—no side trips or unnecessary stopping along the way. He'd been efficient and to the point in getting her settled, letting his superiors and the other enlisted medical officers know that she was there to lend a hand wherever it was needed most. He seemed very well-respected for the most part. And even if he was a bit reserved, he was friendly to almost everyone. It just didn't make a whole lot of sense that he would condone such horrors from his men. If it were true, though, it was just one more reason to make them all pay when she got her brother out of there.

Eli stared at the new doctor. The look he thought he'd seen yesterday was back, and a part of him itched to ask exactly what sort of thoughts were causing such distress. But as before, the look was quickly gone, and the moment passed again without comment.

"Did you want me to go ahead and check on the prisoners?"

The voice from outside had Matt almost on his feet before he remembered the pain. Gasping out loud and gripping the wall tightly to keep from falling back over, he looked out the small dirt-stained window of his cell.

What the hell is she doing here? Damn fool's gonna get us all killed.

Shaking his head, he watched as she walked toward the front of the building. If he was truthful with himself, he would admit that he was impressed. She had done a pretty good job on the disguise, and if he had not seen her dressed that way a thousand times before, he might never have guessed that there was a woman buried somewhere beneath it all. Pity about her hair, though.

"Must have damn near killed her to hack it off like that," he sympathized. "Should have known she would do something like this." He silently kicked himself for not telling Katie and Samuel to lock her up if she even so much as mentioned doing such a thing.

Carefully, he sat himself back on the bed, very aware of the way the bandages were pulling at his stitches and the near blinding pain that was again building in his temple. He could hear Ry talking to some of the other men in the building—the guards and the handful of other prisoners that desperately needed medical attention. He was grateful for the extra bit of time, really. It gave him a precious few moments to compose himself, and he prayed he could keep a firm check on his emotions. He wasn't entirely sure that he wouldn't just grab onto her when she walked through the door and hold on for dear life.

"God help her that she doesn't do the same," he prayed.

~*~

"This is our guest of honor at the moment," Eli said, as the door to Matt's cell opened. "They've patched up the gunshot wound as best they could, but he took a nasty hit to his head, and it's still causing some trouble, so we're keeping a close eye."

Ry was forever grateful that Eli's attention was squarely on Matt, or she would have been done for. Her hands grasped the door frame, knuckles turning white, as her vision darkened to mere pinpricks of light. Swaying slightly, it was all she could do not to pass out. Though it had only been a few days, her brother had lost even more weight from his already malnourished frame, and his pale face was streaked with smeared blood. They may have patched him up, but they hadn't bothered to give him any water to wash up with, and he still sat in his soiled uniform. The garment was ripped and stained, nearly beyond repair, from the battle so recently fought. Appalled, she could only stare at the anguish in his eyes, no longer sure if she could handle looking at the rest of him.

Eli continued into the room, oblivious to the current of emotions surrounding him. "Must be your lucky day," he said mockingly to the man he'd once gone to West Point with. "Got ourselves an extra pair of hands willing to come help us out with you sorry bastards for a while." While it might seem that he was uncaring, the truth was that he hated like hell that they were even in this situation. But too often, with the war being what it was, there was just no help for it. Still, it bothered him, and he'd breathed a huge sigh of relief when he had gotten to camp the previous evening and found that, at least as of yet, no one had seen fit to take out their aggressions on the prisoners.

Rather than rise to the bait, Matt just smiled and nodded at Ry. "Captain Matthew James. I'd stand and salute, but that seems to be more than I can handle at the moment." The grin on his face turned quickly to a grimace as the pain from his wounds continued to plague him. At that point, it was obvious that it was all he could do to sit up straight.

"Well, I've got other business to attend to, so if you are all settled here, I'll leave you to it. Just let the guards know when you leave." Not waiting for a reply, Eli turned and headed out the door, leaving Ry and Matt staring at each other in silence.

"Are you crazy?" Matt whispered, his green eyes flaring with emotion. "I'd get up and strangle you, but it would probably kill me."

Trembling, Ry walked slowly to the bed. "Hush now and let me take a look at you." Setting her bag down, she unwrapped the dirty bandage covering his head. "Oh, your hair!" she cried, her fingers trailing lightly over his partly shaved scalp.

"You're one to talk." He laughed, pointing to her own shorn locks.

"Indeed." She acknowledged the point.

Looking closely at his scalp, she could see why it had been necessary. Head wounds bleed like crazy, and this one was deep enough to have needed stitches. The task now was to keep it clean and hope he hadn't cracked his skull in the process.

"How are you feeling, really?"

"Hurts like hell," he said, opting for the truth. "The head, I think, is the worst of it. Keep getting these pains like someone stabbing a knife through my eye socket."

She washed up the wound area again and rewrapped his head with a clean bandage. "Those should start to subside in a week or two, as long as you rest up," she said soberly. "That's what happens when you knock your brains around like that. Lucky it didn't kill you outright." Shaking her head, she moved down to examine his other wound. "Let's take a look at your side," she said, carefully cutting through the bandages.

Her hands flew to her mouth, stifling a cry of horror at the red, puffy wound. While his head might have been hurting him worse, it was clearly the less serious of the two injuries. "Dear God, you are lucky," she whispered. "Just a bit more to the right…" She left it hanging, unable to give voice to the stark truth.

While she was eternally grateful to the army doctors for getting the bullet out, it was obvious that they had not cared so much about cleanliness when they'd stitched him back up. The infection needed to be contained, and fast. It was a miracle Matt wasn't delirious from fever as it was. "We need to clean this up, then you'll start to feel much better," she said, trying to hide her concern.

"So really, Ry, what exactly are you doing here? I know you didn't ride all the way here just to treat my wounds." Matt spoke softly to keep his words from carrying, but there was real fear in his eyes as he looked at her.

"Taking a walk in the park," she whispered back, her words dripping with sarcasm. "What do you think I'm doing, you idiot?" Agitated, she paced the room. "Not quite sure how yet, but now that I'm here, I'll be able to come up with something. You will need some time to recover from this mess anyways, and that should give me all the time I need. Just concentrate on getting well, you hear!"

Ry put her supplies away and closed up her bag. Cupping his face gently, she kissed his brow. "I've got to go. They will start to wonder if I stay in here any longer. Make sure that you get some rest. I'll be back in tomorrow to check on you again."

For his part, Matt just stared after her. Hard to argue with a woman who didn't let you get a word in edgewise. Still, he was terrified, and if he could have found a way to make her leave without arousing suspicion, he would have done it in an instant. Curling up on his bed, he closed his eyes against the near blinding pain in his head.

"Keep yourself safe, Ry," he whispered.

Ry went out, noting as she left, that the guards on duty had rechecked all cell doors after her, dashing all hope of her being able to just accidentally leave one unlocked. Heading to the building that passed for a mess hall, she grabbed a quick bite of supper then walked back to her bunk. Between being in an unfamiliar place, surrounded by the enemy, and her constant worry for Matt, she'd been unable to sleep much the night before. On edge, she had startled awake at the slightest sound. Now that she had a small measure of weight off her chest, exhaustion was crashing down, and she only just made it to her bed before the darkness claimed her.

In Plain Sight

The piercing screams had Ry up and out the door before she'd barely gotten her overshirt fully buttoned. Henry rifle in hand, she raced toward the sounds, breathing only a slight sigh of relief once she realized they were coming from somewhere other than the makeshift prison. Reaching the edge of the encampment, she stopped short. Clenching her teeth so hard that they scraped together, it took every ounce of will she had not to cry out at the sight. The sounds of at least one other person retching nearby assured her that she wasn't the only one horrified, but before she could raise her rifle, Eli burst into the clearing and fired several warning shots.

"This stops *now!*" he thundered.

"Oh, really? What are you going to do about it, Cap'n? We caught 'em sneaking around out here. Only seems fair that we show him just how dangerous spying on us can be." The soldier laughed maliciously as he kicked the broken and bloodied body at his feet. Ry had been sure the man was already dead, but the Confederate spy groaned weakly at the further abuse.

"Maybe you misunderstood my orders, Private," Eli snarled. "You are done here, unless you want to find yourself facing a court martial. War is bad enough... taking it out on them won't make it any better."

Eli and the private stared each other down, neither so much as blinking, as the silence stretched out around them. For the briefest of moments, Ry thought the younger man might challenge Eli again. She could see the private gauging his chances, but whatever he was, he wasn't nearly as stupid as he looked. Deciding he'd had enough fun for the night, he shrugged and backed off. Motioning for his buddies to follow, the private walked off into the woods without another word.

Ry glanced over at Eli, noting the haunted look in his eyes; the blue having turned to cold steel with barely suppressed anger. Forgetting herself for a moment, she almost reached out to him, wanting to do something, anything to make that look vanish. Eli turned to her then, and the moment was broken.

"Let's get him to the prison infirmary and see if there's anything you can do to help him."

He looked thoroughly sickened as they loaded the soldier carefully onto the stretcher that one of the other soldiers had brought up from the main infirmary. Eli signaled for a couple of other men to help, then they slowly made their way back to the makeshift prison. Racing ahead, Ry cleared a table in the front room, and as soon as they arrived, Eli and his men laid the soldier gently on it.

"Sorry to leave you like this, but I've got to go make sure that everyone settles down." He shook his head wearily. "Just do what you can for him. We'll move him to one of the open cells when you're done. If you need anything else, just tell Davey here." Eli nodded at the young guard to his left as he walked back out into the night.

Ry watched him go then turned to look at the man lying on the table. Reaching over, she carefully pulled open his jacket and finally lost the battle to keep her dinner down. Running for the door, she barely made the porch rail before heaving over the edge.

"Jesus." She wiped her mouth on the back of her sleeve then closed her eyes and took several deep breaths. The chilled air seeped into her lungs as she tried desperately to get her stomach to stop rebelling. Swallowing hard, she slowly regained control of herself and walked back inside.

"Sorry about that." Her voice was still a bit shaky. "I've seen some pretty bad injuries, but… well…" She trailed off, not even able to find the words to describe it. The guards just nodded sympathetically then turned back to keep watch.

"I'll do what I can," she whispered, mostly to herself. "But I don't know that it's going to be enough."

What she really wanted to do was cry. She was only there to get her brother and leave; she shouldn't even have had to treat such horrible injuries. But she knew too, that the Union doctors didn't have a whole lot of time for any of the Confederate boys; they really only concerned themselves with their own. Not that they were inherently cruel, but the sheer number of wounded led them to make tough choices sometimes. And when it came down to it, they would choose the boys in blue before those in gray every time. In her heart, though, Ry knew this man wasn't going to make it, even if she'd had help from the army doctors.

"Dear God! That anyone could do this to another person!" Choking back a sob, she used her fingers to lightly probe the bruised skin.

She continued to work diligently—for hours, it seemed—cleaning up the blood and muck as best she could and trying to stop new bleeding from the half dozen bayonet wounds the soldier had received. Several of them were deep, and so close to his heart that she was amazed he was even still breathing. To her horror, that wasn't even the worst of it. In several places on the man's body it looked as if those torturing him had burned him with fire, searing the very flesh from his bones until it simply oozed away. They'd finished him off with savage kicks and punches, breaking several of his ribs, as they continued to brutalize his body.

She nearly jumped out of her skin when the cold hand closed over her wrist. Looking down at her patient, she realized that his lips were moving. Reaching for a cup and some water, she helped him take a small sip then leaned in closer as he tried to speak again.

"It's all right, ma'am. I know I'm dying."

He whispered it, his voice weak and hoarse with pain, but still she glanced around sharply to see if the guards had heard. Their heads were bent over a small table, and it was clear to Ry that they weren't paying a bit of attention to anything but the card game they'd started to pass the time. Turning back to her patient, she forced a smile to her face and patted his hand reassuringly. "I'm going to do my best to see that you don't." She prayed like hell that he didn't see the lie in her eyes.

His grip tightened on her arm, surprisingly strong considering the shape he was in, forcing her to look at him again as he shook his head. "No, I don't want you to." The words caught in his throat as the exertion of trying to speak took its toll, but still, his eyes held hers. They were bright with pain and fever from the infections already brewing in his body, even so, she could see and hear the conviction behind every word.

"Let me go... please!" he finally begged. "The pain... I'm so tired of fighting."

Whether he was referring to the pain from his wounds or the entirety of the war, she never knew. No longer able to hold back her tears, Ry let them stream down her face as she rummaged in her bag. Grasping the bottle of laudanum, she removed the cap and poured a liberal dose into the cup along with some more water.

"Here, drink this." Her heart hammered in her chest. She couldn't afford to break down, but this was definitely not what she had envisioned when she made her plans to rescue Matt.

"Thank you," he whispered, gulping down the bitter liquid in one shot. "You are my angel of mercy."

His eyes closed as the laudanum took effect, and she continued to clean up his wounds, trying to minimize the damage, though she knew it was all in vain. She may not have been able to save him, but at least she could stay with him and treat him well until the end. Which, judging from the way his breathing had changed, wouldn't be much longer. Keeping a silent vigil, she held his hand in her own, whispering meaningless words of comfort.

After he took his last breath, she took a moment to compose herself, hoping that her grief-ravaged face didn't give her away. Turning away, she packed up her things and walked toward the door. The guards looked up from their game, but she just shook her head.

"Please inform Captain Webb that he didn't make it." Her voice echoed hollowly in her ears. Then without waiting for a response, she continued on out to her quarters.

CHAPTER FIVE

Virginia: November 11, 1863

The sun was streaming through the windows when Ry finally roused herself from sleep. She lay exactly as she had fallen, not even bothering to get under the covers, which was probably a good thing since she was still covered in blood. Dawn had been breaking when she finally stumbled to her bed, and she'd barely made it back before starting to weep uncontrollably. The tears may have stopped, but now she was filled with a numb sense of grief—all for a young man whose name she didn't even know, and never would.

She tried shaking it off, but the loss was still too fresh in her mind. She wanted nothing better than to throw the covers over her head and hide. Knowing, however, that she couldn't lie around in bed all day without arousing suspicion, she tried moving. Watching the dried blood flake off her shirt, she was instantly confronted with the reality that she was going to have to head to the river for a bath.

Up until now, she had been grateful for the cold November weather. In the hotter months of summer, someone might have questioned why she didn't remove her shirt at night in the heat. So cold was good, until she actually needed to plunge her naked body into a freezing river. She shivered violently just thinking about it.

With no other options available, she resigned herself to the unpleasant task ahead. Taking only a quick moment to gather a spare set of clothing, she headed out, thankful at least that with the cold, it was highly unlikely that anyone else would join her—a definite point in her favor, to be sure. Still, when she reached the normally shallow ford just outside the encampment, the churning waters from the recent rains were unappealing at best.

Despite the current conditions, it had always been peaceful there. In summers past, she and Matt had often ridden out this way to cool off with a swim

73

and sleep under the stars. She stood quietly for several moments, lost in thought as the icy waters rushed by, doing her best to prolong the inevitable.

Well… let's get this over with.

Finally girding herself for the icy plunge, she sat down to remove her boots, but then decided that it was best to just leave everything else on. Though it was probably a lost cause, she still needed to try to get the dried blood out of her clothing, plus she would need the extra covering if anyone else happened to come down this way. She definitely couldn't afford to get caught with her pants down. She giggled to herself at the thought despite the deadly seriousness of the situation.

The water very nearly took her breath away. To say it was bone-chilling was putting it mildly. More accurately, it felt like ice-cold needles being driven into her skin. In her younger days, she and Matt would have done this—they actually had done this—as a dare, but her smile at the memories quickly vanished as reality set in. She needed to figure out something soon. This was no place for either of them to linger for too much longer. To do so would only invite disaster to fall on them both.

Deciding at last that she was likely as clean as she would ever be, or at least as clean as she didn't mind being before she turned into a human block of ice, Ry headed back to dry land and quickly removed her dripping clothes.

Being naked left her vulnerable, so she rebound her breasts quickly then threw on a clean shirt. She was just buttoning her pants when she heard the sound of footsteps coming toward her through the trees. Fear coursed through her, and worried of a repeat of the previous night, she reached for her rifle. Easing it back down only at the last moment as she realized that whoever was coming wasn't bothering to be stealthy about it. Standing her ground, she waited. The sound of twigs snapping and leaves crunching were loud in the cool silence of the afternoon.

"How's the water?" Eli was covered in mud again and looked about as excited to jump in the river as she had been.

"Eh... not bad once you get used to it." She sealed off the bald-faced lie with an evil little grin. "I was just finishing up here, so I'll leave you to it."

She started to walk past him, but he reached out his arm to stop her. Heart hammering in her chest, she looked up at him, praying he couldn't see the fear in her eyes.

"Sorry about last night. Most of my men are good men, but there's always a couple of troublemakers in every bunch."

Nearly sighing in relief, she slowly let out the breath she'd been holding. "It's fine. Hopefully, they'll listen to you, and it won't happen again."

She tried to sound reassuring, but in her heart, she knew the only thing that would likely stop those bastards from doing something similar again was death, or near to it. Men like that didn't care about right or wrong. They had probably spent most of their childhood torturing small animals and like as not, had only joined up just so they would have a legitimate reason to move on to bigger prey. She really hoped it wouldn't fall to Eli to serve out their final punishment. He would do it because it was the right thing to do, but she could see too that the whole thing weighed heavily on his shoulders.

Turning away to head back to camp, she realized, most awkwardly, that he still had not moved his arm and was, even now, staring intently at her. Looking up, she could see the confusion in his eyes, and she nearly panicked at the thought that her secret had been discovered. The tension between them was nearly palpable. Despite her resolve and the fact that he was the enemy, there were definite thoughts of swooning the more she got to know him. She could only imagine what sorts of things were going through his head. At least she knew she was a woman, but if he was feeling anything similar, she was quite sure it was probably something he wasn't prepared to deal with— at least not as long as he considered her to be a man.

Not that such things didn't happen. There were camp followers to be sure, but still, when someone spends all their time around other men, it's bound to happen. Unlike most well-bred ladies her age, she wasn't that naive about human nature. The situation would have been almost laughable if there wasn't so much at stake. But in truth, it wasn't worth her brother's life to find out how Eli would react if she kissed her self-described *well-built* captain here and now. Deliberately pulling herself away from him, she broke the spell.

"Enjoy your swim," she said before quickly walking away.

What in the hell was that?

Confusion wasn't exactly how Eli would have described it, though there was definitely some of that too. He really felt as if he was losing his mind. Sure, it had been a rather long time since he'd had a good woman warming his bed, but was that any sort of excuse for nearly kissing another man? He wasn't entirely sure what it was about Ry that kept nagging at him. There was something familiar about the doctor to be sure, a lingering feeling that they had met somewhere before. Reasonable enough, except that Eli wasn't from around these parts at all, having spent most of his time before West Point up in Boston, living with his maternal grandfather. Before that, he resided with his mother and father on their small farm in the mountains of northern Georgia. Until recently, at the most gracious orders of the US Army, he had never even set foot in Virginia, and it wasn't as though he was out doing a lot of socializing now that he was there.

"Damn it all!" he swore.

Then without another thought, he stripped down and took the plunge. He came up spluttering, and any unwanted feelings he might have had were quickly doused by the frigid water streaming down his body. The shocking cold brought his attention firmly to the task at hand. He wasted no time washing up, not wanting to stay in the water a moment longer than he had to. Being clean was nice, but not at the risk of getting pneumonia. Satisfied that he would not disgrace his uniform too much, he climbed out of the river and redressed to ward off the harsh chill that was settling in.

The crisp fall air was sweet and fresh, and in other times, he might have enjoyed the solitude of a walk in the woods. Though the trees had long since lost most of their leaves, there were still a few lone splashes of red and gold—a sharp contrast to the cold, unrelenting gray of the sky. Winter was definitely coming, and from the looks of things, it was promising to be a bad one.

"Just one more thing to deal with," Eli murmured to himself. "God help me, I can't wait for this damn war to be over." Shaking his head in disgust, he left the icy river behind and made his way back to the encampment.

Stopping long enough to hang her sodden clothing and grab her medical bag, Ry went to check on her brother and the other prisoners. Having slept more than half the day away, it was nearing dark as she made her way through the tents, but she didn't want to go a whole day without seeing Matt. He would likely be worried enough as it was, especially after the commotion the night before. Nodding to the guards as she entered, she went in to see her first patient.

Desperate as she was to see her brother, she didn't want to draw any undue attention to herself by rushing to his room. With her nerves stretched thin, she made herself check on the others first. Thankfully, they all seemed to be doing well and would soon be in good enough shape to be moved to the regular prison camps. Wishing that she could let them all go, she buried those thoughts down deep inside her heart, knowing it was going to be difficult, at best, just to get her brother out. It was a hard truth, but like the soldier last night, she couldn't save everyone, no matter how much she might have wanted to.

Finally, she opened the door to Matt's cell. He was still sitting on the bed, but his color was better, and his breathing seemed much steadier.

"How are the headaches today?" she asked, trying to keep a professional tone.

"Not as bad, but still a little rough. Side is feeling better too," he answered, matching her tone.

"I'll be the judge of that. Let me take a look." Peeling back the bandages under his ribs, she was pleased to see that the wound was less angry-looking than it had been just the day before. With any luck, Matt would be able to move in about a week. The only thing to do now was figure out exactly how to get him out, and more importantly, not get caught before then.

Ostensibly checking his head wound, Ry leaned over and whispered softly. "I'm still working on the escape plan. There's only the two guards on the building, but we're in the dead center of everything, so even if you get out the door…" She left it hanging.

"Let's just say, we're going to need one hell of a distraction to make this work. Not sure what yet, but you still need at least a few more days to heal up, so I'm sure I will come up with something before then." She smiled and ruffled what little bit was left of his hair.

Other than begging her to leave him behind for the sake of her own safety, there was nothing Matt could say. So he simply nodded, staring mutely at her face. He could plainly see the toll this charade was taking on Ry, and it pained him ever so much that he was the cause of it all.

"I was worried about you last night," he said, finally finding his voice. "All that screaming. At first, I thought it was you, and it was all I could do not to go crazy, but then I heard you in the other room." His voice was thick with emotion as he reached out to touch her cheek. "Please be careful. It's not worth your life to get me out of here. I couldn't live with that. So if you don't see any way to get us both clear, then you need to just leave." He held her gaze, willing her to really listen to his words. "I'll heal up and take my chances. Odds are they'll do a prisoner exchange or something, anyway. Ain't like they'll really want another mouth to feed with winter coming on."

Though he'd said it with a tone of absolute conviction, Matt knew she could see the uncertainty in his eyes. If Ry left him there, he would likely never see her again, and they both knew it.

"Hush up, you!" she said. "I'm not leaving without you, so just you forget about trying to make me." Hastily wiping at the tears that threatened to spill over, she tidied up and headed for the door. "I'll see you tomorrow."

The guards were playing cards again, clearly a common pastime, and this time they barely grunted as she walked past. "Well, at least they're diligent at something," she mumbled, laughing to herself as her mood finally lightened a bit. Her stomach growled loudly, reminding her that it had been a good twenty-four hours since she had last had any food. Looking for a way to remedy the gnawing emptiness in her belly, she went off in search of a bite to eat.

The mess hall was fairly crowded, and she was surprised anyone could even hear themselves think over the dull roar that emanated from the enclosed space. Steaming bowl of stew in hand, she started to wade through the men to find a place to sit and eat her meal. However, when she saw Eli heading her way again, she changed her mind and walked back out into the night. It would be quieter in her quarters and safer. Much safer.

Eli noticed the change in direction and wondered if Ry was purposefully avoiding him. Though to be fair, after the way he'd acted this afternoon it wasn't as if he could really expect anything different.

Grabbing a plate, he headed back to his quarters. With the messages he'd received earlier, he now had some serious planning to do. As much as he liked having a solid roof over his head, it looked as though he was going to have to get used to riding out again. At least half his men would be heading straight toward Culpeper to join up with General Meade, and thankfully, they would be taking the prisoners with them.

Though the rest of them would stay on in their current location for a bit longer, getting even half an army ready to move out was always a nightmare, so he might as well start working on the details. He would be meeting up with the major and the other officers in the morning, and they would expect him to have everything figured out before then. Why they thought he was any better than anyone else at these sorts of things he'd never really understood, but somehow the details were always left up to him.

Leaving the encampment meant leaving Ry behind as well, but at this point, that was probably a good thing. Still, the extra set of skilled hands would be sorely missed. Even more so because Eli knew that once he was gone, any seriously wounded enemy his men came across would likely die before they got any sort of critical medical care. It's not that the doctors under his command were outright hateful or uncaring, but as Ry herself had previously noted, they had their priorities. Unfortunately, treating the enemy just wasn't at the top of that list.

He continued to stare at the papers in front of him for several minutes, eyes unseeing as the exhaustion stole over him. When he caught his head drooping toward his chest for the third time, he finally gave up, knowing all too well he would get nothing else accomplished in his fatigued state. Besides, it was better to rest up now as he wouldn't be getting any sleep soon enough. He moved to his bed, climbed in and then, without another thought, drifted off to sleep.

CHAPTER SIX

Virginia: November 13, 1863

Though the weather stayed clear, the temperatures turned downright frigid, and most mornings they woke to a thin layer of frost coating everything that wasn't covered. Ry's daily routine was fairly standard—get up, make rounds, stay out of everyone else's way, go to bed, get up, and do it all again. So far, the soldiers had given her no indication that they suspected her of anything other than wanting to be helpful. Nonetheless, Ry's nerves were stretched tighter than a violin's strings by the end of the week; one wrong twist, and she feared they would simply snap. While she knew full well that Matt needed the time to rest up, the waiting was likely going to kill her. Worse, despite thinking about it from every possible angle, she had yet to figure out exactly how the hell to get them out of this mess.

Getting him out of the cell would be easy enough, but the rest... not so much. There was one small chance, but getting Matt to agree was going to take some really fast talking. Even then, without some sort of major distraction, the plan was still destined to fail. Gathering her courage, she headed over to the prison building. She knew he would object, but they had no other choice, at least not as far as she could see. She was welcome there; Eli had long-since smoothed over any misgivings that anyone might have had about her. Hell, no one even paid any attention to her any more. At this point, she could probably come and go as she pleased if she wanted to. So if she could just get Matt out first, it would be easy enough to follow when all the commotion had died down. All that was really left was to devise a distraction that couldn't be tracked back to her.

"Should be easy as pie," she muttered, rolling her eyes.

"You want to do *what*?" Matt's voice was deceptively calm, barely above a whisper, but his icy gaze told the real story.

"You heard me," she said. "When it's time, I want you to knock me out. Well... pretend to, anyways, then head for home as fast as you can. When I'm found, I'll act all apologetic and offer to help hunt you down if necessary. In any case, within a couple of days after things have settled back down, I'll follow you home."

She said it matter-of-factly, knowing that he would have to give in eventually. Still, he protested vehemently, just as she'd known he would.

"You are utterly out of your mind if you think I'm going to leave here without you. Seriously"—he grasped her arm—"there has to be another way." His eyes held hers, the silence stretching between them, as he willed her to give up on her craziness.

Breaking away, she shook her head. "I wish there was, but I've racked my brain, and this is it. So, unless you can come up with something better..." She left the thought hanging. "I mean, I don't want to stay here any longer than I have to, but I just don't see that we have any other options."

She stood and paced, dropping all pretense of wound-checking for the moment. "If we both go, they might start asking questions that could lead back to home, and I don't want to put Katie or Samuel in any danger. At least if it's only you, then it's just a lone Confederate soldier who didn't quite like the idea of spending the remainder of the war in a Union prison camp. Can't no one blame you for that one."

He nodded. "Oh, I see the logic of it, but it still doesn't mean that I have to like it any." He sighed, reaching out to twine his fingers through hers. "You are taking way too many risks for me, and I'm just not sure that it's worth it."

Appalled, she could only stare at him. "Of course, it's worth it, you ninny!" She smacked him lightly. "Seriously, though, you are all that I have left, and I'm not going to lose you. And that's the end of it."

He started to object again, but the look in her eye was one he knew all too well—she meant what she said. It would be a waste of breath to even try. Sighing, he resigned himself to the inevitable. "So when are we doing this?"

"Not sure yet, but hopefully within the next couple of days. The rumor is that they will be moving out of here soon, so definitely before then." She looked at him appraisingly. "I know you could use a lot more rest, but I don't think you're in any real danger of keeling over if you have to exert yourself for short periods of time. Just be ready; I might not be able to give much notice."

He grinned. "Aye, aye, Captain."

She had missed his smile, and it eased her heart to see that he still had a bit of silliness in him. Unfortunately, there were too many others who would likely never laugh again.

"Okay, I'm going," she said. "See you tomorrow."

"Love you, Ry," he whispered, as she turned to leave.

The shots echoed through the encampment, and again, Ry found herself out the door, rifle in hand, before she was barely aware of what was going on.

Eli raced by her, pausing only long enough to shout a quick warning. "We're under attack. Stay back and out of the way."

"I'll go set up and be ready for any wounded prisoners," she shouted before turning back to her bunk to grab her bag. Her thoughts raced ahead as she revised her plans. *Guess I won't be needing that distraction after all. Now to just get rid of the guards.*

She hurried down the street, dodging the soldiers that were running in the opposite direction toward the fighting. From the sounds of it, they were being hit from both the south and west sides. Running up the steps, she slowed as she entered the prison building, trying hard to catch her breath. After a quick glance inside, she smiled briefly, trying without much success to keep from full-on grinning. For once, there was only one guard on duty.

"Got to get ready in case there are any wounded," she said to him as she passed, her emotions firmly back under control. He simply nodded and went back to watching the door. No card game tonight. Young Davey was all business—on high alert, gun at the ready for any sign of trouble. Ignoring him for the moment, Ry went to work, going through the motions of clearing the table and setting out some basic supplies.

Without warning, a mortar round exploded nearby, and the blast nearly knocked Ry off her feet. Ears ringing, she used the wall to steady herself. Glancing around to make sure the guard's attention was elsewhere, she used the confusion to knock a quick pattern on the wall connected to Matt's cell.

"He better recognize that," she mumbled under her breath. "Not like we didn't use it all the time as kids, but still, it's been a long time."

Going back to the table, she made an effort to look busy, but she needn't have worried. Matt's answering groan came within minutes, and to anyone listening, it sounded for all the world like he was dying.

"Oh… he was doing so well the last few days," she complained to Davey. "Guess I better go check on him. I'll be right back."

He barely acknowledged her, his entire focus on the skirmishes outside the door. Grabbing the keys to Matt's cell, she walked down the hallway to unlock the door.

He was curled up on his bed and still groaning. For a brief moment, Ry thought he had truly relapsed. When she rushed over to him, he turned his face to her and grinned.

"Oh… you!" She glared at him, smacking his arm for good measure.

"Wasn't sure if one of the guards was with you, so figured it would be better to at least look as bad off as I sounded," he said. "Sorry it worried you."

His look of concern was endearing, and she gave in gracefully. "No, really, it was good thinking." She gave his bandages a last-minute check.

He had removed the gauze from his head, having done his best to cover the glaring bald spot where they'd shaved him. It didn't look great, but hopefully between the darkness and chaos of the attack, no one would notice.

"Well, it's now or never. You ready?" She tried hard to steady her nerves.

"As I'll ever be," Matt replied. "Are you?"

She nodded, determined to see this through, despite the fears that threatened to cripple her. "There is one guard on the door. You will need to take him down, but it shouldn't be too much of a problem, though. He's not much more than a boy." She sighed, shaking her head, "Jesus, kids that young should still be at home with their mothers."

The enormity of what they were about to do was very nearly her undoing, and she closed her eyes briefly, letting everything drift away. When she felt the calm descend, she opened them again. She could still feel the slight tremble in her legs, but at least it was under control now.

Taking a deep breath, she continued. "You'll need to head north when you get out, keeping as far away as you can from the main fighting to the south and west. I'd make sure to find good cover during the day and travel only at night. Still shouldn't take more than two, maybe three days for you to reach home. Don't push yourself unless you have to. I'll follow as soon as I can." She hugged him tight then stepped back, fearing that if she didn't let go now, she never would.

"Stay safe." He wanted to say more but knew in his heart they had more than passed the point for words by now.

"You too. Now, hit me!" She knew how to brace herself for the punch. They had fought many a

97

time growing up, and he'd taught her well. Still, the pain was worse than she remembered, and she went down hard.

Matt hesitated only long enough to make sure she was okay. He gave her hand one last squeeze then slipped into the hall. Glancing around the corner, he could see the guard and noted that Ry's assessment of his age was dead-on. Poor kid didn't look more than fifteen, if even that.

Thankfully, though, he was still more concerned with the potential threats from outside, so he never saw the one from inside coming at him. Running silently across the room, Matt grabbed Davey from behind. Before the boy could even get a shout out, he was hit with a solid punch that knocked him out cold.

Praying he hadn't done any lasting damage, Matt grabbed the guard's blue wool coat and his gun then headed out the door. The coat was ill-fitting—how not when Matt was a good five inches taller and nearly twice as broad—and he heard a seam split as he put it on. Still, it was enough to give the illusion of belonging. Keeping to the shadows as much as possible and taking care not to draw attention to himself, he walked purposefully toward the waiting woods.

As the sounds of fighting slowly faded behind him, Matt sighed in relief, sparing a glance back the way he'd just come. "You better get out soon, Ry, or there will be hell to pay." Picking up the pace, he headed for home.

For as long as she could, Ry lay motionless and silent on the cold, hard floor. The rough, splintered wood pressed against her cheek as the minutes turned to hours, stretching out before her until she thought she would go mad with the waiting. But as the sounds of battle started receding, she knew it was only a matter of time before someone found them. Reaching up, she ran her fingers gingerly over the lump that was forming on the side of her head, noticing belatedly that she was actually bleeding.

"Thanks a lot," she whispered, wincing in pain. "Definitely going to have to pay you back for that one when I get home."

Moving slowly and leaning heavily on the bed, she sat up. She was going to have a blinding headache in the morning, but it was all worth it if Matt made it out. Struggling to her feet, she took a deep breath, willing the nausea to subside. Then, pale and shaking, she stumbled to the door and down the hallway. "Guess I need to practice my falls better," she muttered to herself. She might have laughed, but in truth, it hurt a bit too much at the moment.

She had almost made it to the front room, when there was a shout from porch. "Bring him in and set him on the table."

Ry's heart slammed in her chest as the remaining blood drained from her face. She nearly ran into Eli as she turned the corner. *God, please don't let it be Matt... please!*

Taking one look at her appearance, Eli immediately went on alert. "What the hell happened here? I told you to stay out of the way!"

His tone was harsh, and her mouth went dry as she grasped for the right words. To be sure, she was still playing her part, but the fear was real, and it gave her just the edge she needed to sound convincing.

"Dunno…" She pressed her hand to her head for greater effect. "Prisoner… thought he'd relapsed. He was moaning and groaning like he was dying. Next thing I know, I'm waking up on the floor," she stammered.

She could see Davey still on the floor, just starting to come around. "I should see to him," she said, holding onto the wall to keep from falling over. Eli just stared at her, his eyes taking in every single detail. Despite her fear, she endured his scrutiny, letting her injured face speak for itself. He would either believe or he wouldn't, but she had to keep moving or she would go crazy waiting for the hammer to fall.

Breaking the spell, she motioned to Eli as she moved to help Davey to the nearest chair. "Help me get him up. As soon as I'm done here, I'll get to the one on the table." Her head was spinning, but she switched into professional mode. Ignoring the pain, she buried all her worries and fears, letting the work take her away. Only the slight shake of her hands gave evidence that she was barely holding on.

She gave Davey a once-over, thankful there didn't seem to be any major injuries, though like her, he was probably going to have one hell of a headache for the rest of the night. Eli was questioning him closely, but she could feel his eyes on her, watching every move she made.

"Did you see anything unusual before you were attacked?" he asked.

"No sir, was just me and the doc here." Davey's voice trembled slightly, either from pain or fear; it was hard to tell. "Prisoner started carrying on after the big explosion, only made sense for Doc to go check on him." Poor kid looked as though he was going to cry, and she felt guilty for putting him in that position.

Eli turned briefly to her, and she nodded in confirmation. "It never occurred to me that anything was amiss." She did her best to look apologetic. "I'm really sorry. If I hadn't opened the cell, this would have never happened." She wasn't sure if Eli was buying it or not, but he seemed to have run out of questions, at least for the moment.

"All right, you finish up here. I need to go help make sure that everything is secure and see about getting a tracker or two on our escapee." He sighed, his body slumping with exhaustion. "What a night." He shook his head then turned and left the building.

It took a supreme effort on her part not to let the breath she was holding whoosh out all at once, though judging by the look on Davey's face, Ry needn't have bothered. Clearly, he was feeling just the same, even if it was for entirely different reasons.

"You let me know if the pain in your head gets too bad, you hear," she said to him, patting him on the shoulder sympathetically.

He nodded and slowly made his way back across the room to his post by the door, determined to make up for his earlier lapse. Watching him, she noticed there was a second guard on duty again, a definite sign they weren't going to take any other chances with the prisoners they had left.

She still felt bad about not letting the others go as well—it was something she and Matt had discussed hurriedly before he'd left. The decision had been a hard one to make, but in truth, there was just no plausible way she could have explained five other open cells. At least not without being immediately thrown into one of her own, with the door locked up tight behind her. As much as Matt hated to leave some of his fellow soldiers behind, the price of setting them free wasn't one he'd been willing to pay.

Wishing she could have followed Eli out the door, she ran a hand over her face, attempting to clear away the mind-numbing fog that was settling over her. She needed to finish up quickly, or her body was simply going to shut down. "Well then, let's see what we have here." She turned to the patient on the table.

Whoever it was, they were still out cold, which was just as well, considering the amount of time it had taken her to get around to looking at him. "Surface injuries look minor… that's a good sign." She said the words out loud. Though no one was really listening, talking her way through his injuries helped to keep her focused on the task at hand. Running her hands carefully over his arms and legs, she checked for broken bones. "Oh, but that's a nasty bruise there on your temple. Almost matches mine, though I'm guessing you got hit a lot harder than I did from the way you're still snoozing away." With a worried frown, she completed her assessment then shook her head. "Not much else I can do for you at this point but let you sleep it off and hope you wake up in the morning."

Though she hated to bother either one of the guards, she motioned for them both. "Can one of you help me move him into a cell, please?"

The new guard turned with a grunt. He was more than twice the size of Davey, and looking closely, Ry felt her heart drop like a stone in her chest as she recognized the private from her first night in the encampment. Of all the people she did not want to be around, this man was at the top of her list. She was a little surprised Eli would have put him on guard duty at the prison. Given his vicious nature and his clear hatred of the enemy, it just didn't make a whole lot of sense, but at least on this night, he didn't seem to have any plans other than keeping watch.

Without a word, he walked over and picked the prisoner up, not even bothering to wait for her to help. Throwing the man unceremoniously over his shoulder, he took him to the cell just opposite of the one Matt had recently vacated.

"Careful. He probably shouldn't be jostled like..." The words died in her throat as the guard stared her down, his cold, dead eyes boring into her soul.

Even in silence, he made it perfectly clear that he didn't care what condition the patient was in. To prove his point, he dropped the prisoner on the bed like a sack of potatoes. Then he looked at her again.

"You were saying?" His tone dared her to open her mouth again.

Ry winced but held her ground, knowing that if she showed even the slightest hint of fear, she would be done for. "Nothing important. Thank you for your help." She said it with a smile, as if he had been the most perfect of gentlemen.

His expression never changed. He simply jerked his arm toward the door, motioning her to leave. Giving the prisoner a last look, she made sure he was settled as best as he could be, then she followed the guard out of the cell.

They walked back to the front room in silence, and Ry was feeling down enough by now that she would have left it at that, but it wouldn't have looked right if she didn't at least try to do her job properly. "You will need to check on him every so often, please. If he worsens, call me, and I will come see what I can do."

The guard just grunted at her again, not that she had really expected much else, but Davey nodded. "Will do."

"Thank you."

As she headed down the street, she was startled to see that daylight was already breaking through the trees. "There goes another sleepless night." She sighed as her shoulders slumped with exhaustion.

"Sleep is highly overrated." Eli's voice came from right behind her.

"Jesus, you shouldn't sneak up on a person like that!" Her heart hammered loudly in her chest. She hoped she had managed to keep the trembling out of her voice but wasn't entirely sure she had succeeded.

"Sorry about that," he said. "Was heading to the mess hall and saw you standing there. Didn't realize you didn't hear me coming."

At the mention of food, Ry's stomach growled. "Oh... umm... food sounds good." She tried to cover her embarrassment. Her cheeks were on fire, and she prayed he couldn't see the color rising in the early morning light.

"Guess you haven't eaten in a while, either," he said with a grin. "Let's go eat."

Not seeing any way to avoid it without it looking suspicious, Ry nodded. "Sure, sounds great."

CHAPTER SEVEN

Virginia: November 14, 1863

From the way Ry attacked her food, one would have thought it was a bowl of the Gods' own ambrosia rather than the half-rotten field rations served by the US Army. Under normal circumstances, she probably wouldn't have even fed this stuff to her pigs, but her sporadic eating schedule made for a powerfully tasty sauce. She tried unsuccessfully to slow herself down, but in truth, she had nearly licked the bowl clean before Eli got around to eating more than a few spoonfuls of his meal.

Blessedly, he chose to ignore her voracious appetite. "How's your head?" he asked between bites.

"Huh? Oh... yeah... umm... not too bad really, all things considered." She gingerly touched the small knot that had formed near her hairline. "Speaking of which, we'll need to keep watch on the prisoner you brought in. His lump was a bit more serious, and at this point, he will be lucky if he wakes up." She shook her head. "Didn't show any signs of movement or make any sounds during treatment, even when we moved him to his cell. Definitely not looking all that good for him."

Eli nodded. "When that blast hit, he wasn't in the direct path but still close enough that the shock of it threw him up against the wall pretty hard. The rest of his boys managed to make it back out, but he was out cold. Guess they thought he was already dead, or they just didn't want to take any chances either way."

She rested with her head in her hands as the exhaustion took over, and he fell silent as he continued to eat his stew. Looking up, she noticed that he was watching her again, and she was reminded what a bad idea it was for her to be anywhere near him, especially now that she was so close to being able to get out of there. Knowing it was the poorest of excuses but being too tired to come up with anything better, she sat up suddenly and winced in pain.

"Ugghh." She grimaced, holding a hand to her stomach. "Think I ate too fast."

His eyes narrowed at the lie, but for the moment, he ignored it. "Gulping down your food when you haven't had much to eat recently is never a good idea. You of all people should know that."

"Yeah, I know. But my belly wasn't listening at the time." She grinned weakly then, still clutching her belly, pushed her chair back from the table. "Well, if you'll excuse me, I think I'm going to go get a few hours of shut-eye."

"Have a good morning," he said curtly, as she rose to leave.

"You too."

Trying her best not to run for it, she made a steady beeline for the door, making doubly sure to keep up the pretense of not feeling well. "Let them think I'm about to be violently ill or something for all I care," she murmured to herself. Which as the panic set in, she realized that wasn't really all that far from the truth. Like as not, she wouldn't feel any better until she was well and far away from this place.

Eli watched Ry leave. The slightly puzzled look on his face was starting to become almost the norm for their encounters. The bellyache had been faked, that was clear enough. The only real question was why? It wasn't as though there was much the doc could do if someone knocked him a good one, especially when he wasn't expecting it. Talk about a case of no good deed going unpunished. Not that Eli could really blame the prisoner, either. He would have likely done the same if their positions had been reversed.

He was just so damn tired, especially after tonight's raid, and all he wanted to do was sleep for a solid week. But in light of everything, he would need to get his men moving sooner rather than later. He definitely couldn't risk having those boys come back again while they were in the middle of packing up.

In his mind, he ran through the various things he would need to change in order to speed up their plans to move out, and with a sigh, he accepted the inevitable. Though he was pushing his own limits, one more night without sleep wasn't likely to kill him, but leaving the army to linger there much longer very well could. In the end, there was really no choice, so he pushed the exhaustion away and focused on the day ahead.

Thankfully, there hadn't been too many wounded in the night's attack, and except for the newest prisoner, none of his own men's injuries were all that severe. "Few stitches here and there, and they will be up and ready to go," or so his own doctors had said. He hoped like hell they were right.

While he wasn't looking forward to having a diminished force, he knew that with a smaller number of men, it would be much easier for them to move around quickly. With any luck, they could eliminate some of the hit-and-run raiding the enemy was doing in the area. It was also expected that he would spend some time tracking the escapee, though honestly, as long as the man went home and stayed there, Eli would be perfectly happy just to leave it as a lower priority on his list.

He sighed again. "Too bad my superiors likely won't see it the same way." Lost in thought, Eli poked at his food, which had gone cold. Without bothering to finish it, he got up and headed out to meet with the other officers.

Ry had most of her gear packed up and ready to go—what little there was of it. Her original plan of sticking it out a few more days no longer seemed like such a great idea, and she was beginning to wish she'd left with her brother. To be sure, no one seemed to be taking his escape all that seriously, but every hour that she stayed felt like another nail in her coffin.

"You're just imagining things, Ry," she told herself, not for the first time. If Captain Webb suspected anything—hell, if anyone suspected—they would have grabbed her up immediately.

She paced the room, trying to calm herself. She had slept maybe an hour or two at most, but then she had been right back up again despite the mind-numbing exhaustion. At the rate she was going, she was truly going to make herself sick. Figuring that she was already more than halfway there, she walked outside to try to clear her head. Standing with her eyes closed, she inhaled the brisk November air, wrinkling her nose as the noxious camp odors invaded her senses.

She laughed, shaking her head. "So much for that idea." Still, it had put her in a better mood, which had to count for something.

Glancing around for the first time, she noticed a veritable ocean of activity around her. Not that the soldiers here were ever idle, but there was a definite difference to their movements, more purposeful.

Taking a closer look, she could see in the distance that the edges of the encampment had already started to come down.

"Guess after last night, they're going to head out to somewhere safer," she mused. "Perfect timing for me. Silly thing, you were worried for nothing." Giddy with relief, she went back inside to bide her time. Thankful that her nerves were somewhat more settled, she let herself doze, getting as much rest as she could before it would be safe to head out.

Several hours later, Ry awoke to the sound of knocking and found Eli standing just outside her door.

"Sorry to bother you," he said. "Wanted you to check on the prisoners one last time before we move them out." He hesitated a moment then continued. "Wanted to find out, too, what your plans are? The bulk of my men are headed up to join General Meade for the winter. Probably won't see too much action, but you're welcome to go as well. They can always use the extra help." He paced the floor, full of nervous energy, as he waited for her reply.

"I'll think about it," she said finally, making a fairly good show of considering the offer. "May head back home for a few days just to check in before going that way. Don't really like to be away for too long with things the way they are." She tried to make it sound as though it was no big deal, but in truth, she had been afraid he was going to order her to go with his men. Despite not actually being in the army, she didn't think that it would matter. If he had wanted to keep an eye on her, he would have pressed her to stick around.

"Either way." He shrugged. "Some of us will still be around here for a bit longer as well. Though we won't be spending near as much time in camp, and we definitely won't have the same luxuries we do now once the main force is gone."

The last was said with a laugh, but she knew what he meant. While it might not seem like much, having a tent or even a dilapidated building for shelter was like paradise compared to sleeping on the cold, hard ground.

"You better get used to cooking your own meals again." She grinned, glancing up at the last moment to see the answering smile cross his face.

Looking at him was a mistake. She knew it immediately but had been unable to help herself. God, she could get lost in his eyes. They were blue like the seas and just as bottomless. His smile faded, and his beautiful eyes darkened with emotion. There was a pulse throbbing in his neck, and she imagined running her tongue slowly across it, tasting the saltiness of his skin. Mesmerized, she could see his hand reaching out for her, his fingers poised to touch her cheek or her hair. Her breath caught in her chest, and even as she swayed toward him, yearning for the smallest contact, her mind frantically screamed at her. She jerked back, eyes wide with shock.

Silently, they stared at each other for a moment longer, then desperately trying to cover for both of them, she turned and walked away. "I'll go check on those men for you."

The words tumbled out in a rush, but she didn't stop to hear if he responded, and she didn't dare look back, much too afraid of what she would see on his face.

For his part, Eli just stood there, staring after her as she walked away, too stunned to even begin to comprehend what had just happened.

"Stupid… stupid… stupid!"

Like a mantra, Ry repeated it over and over as she walked away. "Get in, get these men checked, and get out of here. That's all you have to do; now do it." Doing her best to keep it together, she made her rounds, barely acknowledging the guards on duty other than to note they were back to playing cards. Once inside, she was happy to see that not only were her regular patients still on the road to recovery, but the newest prisoner was conscious when she checked on him as well.

"Nice to see you're awake," she said as she rechecked the swelling. "How are you feeling?"

"Hurts like the dickens, but don't seem to be nothing else broken," he replied. "Thanks for patching me up."

She nodded. "Guess you should rest if you can. They will likely be moving you all soon enough. Even so, try to take it easy as much as possible, at least for the next few days."

Taking her leave, she noticed that one of the guards—the same one who had been less than helpful earlier that morning—was checking the cell doors behind her again. Satisfied that everyone was still locked up like they should be, he followed her out to the porch.

"You better hope you had nothing to do with what happened here last night," he said, breaking the silence. "If I find out different, I will hunt you down."

The threat hung in the air, and Ry wanted nothing more than to protest her innocence or better yet, run away as fast as she could. Of course, that was exactly what he wanted her to do, so she forced herself to stand fast and meet his penetrating gaze.

"Of course." She shrugged. "Wouldn't expect you to do anything less."

It was useless to say much else, so she left. Stopping only briefly at the mess hall to grab some extra rations to help get her through the next couple of days, Ry made her way back to her quarters. Taking a last look around the dingy little room, she grabbed her gear and headed for home, hoping like hell no one else stopped her on the way out.

Eli was helping his men load up the last of the supply wagons when he saw the lone figure slip through the trees. He wasn't entirely sure how he felt about it. He was partially relieved, of course, because then maybe he could finally get his emotions back under control. But rather surprisingly, the urge to race after Ry was strong.

"God, my priorities are screwed up," he mumbled to himself, running a hand through his hair. "If anything, I should be dragging him back just to find out why he's sneaking out like a thief. Though really, who can blame him? I'm actually in the army, and I want to sneak off." It bothered Eli, though, and he worried at it while he worked, still not convinced that he wasn't missing something big.

"Captain?" The soldier's voice jerked him out of his thoughts.

Staring at his lieutenant, he realized that the wagon was all loaded and the men were waiting for their final orders. "Sorry about that. It's been a long couple of days." He shrugged and pointed to the map, addressing the rest of his men. "You all will follow the main road here, then at the split, take the northern fork toward Culpeper. General Meade is camping up that way for the winter and you will be joining up with him for the time being. You'll want to get there as soon as you can, but don't rush and don't take any chances. We'll try to keep any stray enemy raiders off your back until you're out of the area." He saluted his men then watched as they rode off, joining the mass exodus as the other companies moved out as well.

The silence that remained in their wake was almost deafening. Nevertheless, after being surrounded by several hundred Union troops for the last few weeks, Eli more than welcomed the peace and quiet.

He turned back to his lieutenant. "I could definitely get used to this."

"I hear ya, Captain," Cam replied. "But don't think they're going to give us too much time to enjoy it."

Eli nodded. He started to comment, but the exhaustion finally hit him full force. "Well, let's take advantage of it while we can. Tell the men to rest up; we'll start riding patrols early in the morning." Then, knowing that the marching army was safe enough for the time being, he headed off to catch a few much-needed hours of sleep.

CHAPTER EIGHT

Virginia: November 15, 1863

Eternally grateful for the break in the weather, Ry made good time as she ran through the sun-dappled woods. With the army on the move in the opposite direction, she had little to fear in being followed, but still, she stayed alert for the slightest indication that something was amiss. Yet, despite all her precautions, she had been out of the compound for somewhat less than a full day when she heard them coming. Ironically, she was very near to the place where she had first rescued Captain Webb from the Confederate deserters.

"Seems like forever ago," she mused, noting that in fact it had only been little over a week ago that her life had been completely turned upside down. "But I accomplished what I set out to do. That's all that matters. Well, I will have… if I can just make it home."

She glanced to her right, and even through the sparse trees at the edge of the woods, she could see the dust cloud being kicked up in the distance. They weren't right on her, but it would be a close one. Briefly, she lamented not borrowing a horse, but the thought of being branded a horse thief had been more than enough to put an end to any of those sorts of thoughts. They would have come after her for sure if she'd done anything that stupid. Saving her feet a bit of aching definitely wasn't worth the risk.

Shaking her head, she willed her inner dialogue to silence, and focused on her surroundings as she reached the property line. Unfortunately, as Eli had noted before, the fallow fields in front of her offered very little in the way of cover, and despite the coming of night, it was not an area that she wanted to be stuck in while looking for a place to hide. Glancing back again at the cloud of dust, she figured she had just enough time to get across the field if she ran for it. So, without waiting around to see exactly who was following her, she picked up her pace and made for the safety of the trees on the other side.

Old, gnarled, and poking haphazardly from the nearly frozen soil, the hidden root likely saved her life, even if slamming into the cold, hard ground was a less than welcome surprise. Face in the dirt, she lay there for several long moments, sucking in air and desperately trying to catch the breath that had been so painfully knocked from her chest. The troops, whichever side they were on, had made much better time than she'd anticipated and were almost on top of her. Even so, she had very nearly made it to the safety of the waiting darkness. She likely would have too, if the small force of Confederate raiders hadn't burst from the trees directly in front of her, guns blazing. It was only sheer, dumb luck that she was still alive to witness the horror erupting around her. Staying down low, she crawled slowly toward the tree line that lay only about fifty yards in front of her.

She bit back a cry as a body fell to her left, and she saw the wide staring eyes of the young guard who'd been unlucky enough to be on duty the night she had helped her brother escape.

"Oh, Davey, you should have been at home with your mother," she whispered, the tears falling freely down her face as she reached out to gently close his eyes. He had been so kind to her, even when others hadn't, and she was not surprised at the genuine grief she felt at his passing.

Taking a deep breath, she buried her emotions then continued moving, praying she did not find anyone else she knew. *Despite it all, I just don't think I could bear it.* She did not say his name, but an image of Eli's face filled her mind, and for a moment, she thought she was still dreaming when she heard his voice call loudly from across the field.

"Come on, boys! Form up! Cam, take Dalton and Vic; see if you can get around 'em and come from the back."

"Yes, Cap'n!" The reply came from a distance, the men obeying his orders unhesitatingly.

Fear gripped Ry's heart in a painful vise. She was torn between the need to save her own skin and the thought that if she left, Eli would end up just as dead and cold as young Davey. In the end, her own hesitation was her undoing. The horse's hoof clipped the top of her shoulder hard as it thundered past, jumping over her at the last second, recognizing— even if its rider had not—that there had been an obstacle in its path. It was her own fault that she had raised her body up off the ground at exactly the same moment to take another look in Eli's direction.

"Son of a bitch!" The curse escaped her lips before she could stop it. Taking a moment to catch her breath, she gingerly moved her arm, gritting her teeth against the throbbing pain. Nothing seemed broken, but it was surely going to be a sore one.

Taking a bit more care, she began to crawl across the field again, stopping from time to time when the pain became unbearable. The short distance she had left to go suddenly felt like miles, as her body rebelled against the added abuse. In despair, she rested her head on the ground, trying to gather up the strength to continue moving.

In time, the sounds of battle—so heated at first—dwindled into nothingness. It was clear that someone was winning, or hell, maybe they were all losing; it was so hard to tell any more. Sickened by the pain and death around her, Ry was no longer sure of anything. Dredging up the last of her reserves, she finally reached the tree line and glanced back at the field in horror. Bodies lay everywhere. Despite the chaos and destruction they'd caused in the field, both forces were relatively small ones, but even so, the Confederates had been a much larger one than their

Union counterparts. However, as her brother had taught her long ago, bigger wasn't always better, and the fact that the Confederate raiders had been less experienced and disorganized was readily apparent in the grizzly scene before her.

Someone had put a torch to the dried weeds along the south edge of the field, and a harsh orange glow lit up the night sky. Through the smoke and flames, Ry felt as if she was catching a glimpse of Hell itself.

"You'd think they'd just give up," she whispered, watching the last remaining gray coats continue their hopeless assault on the men in blue. "So senseless to just throw your life away like that."

The nudge to her back nearly sent her to her knees from the pain. Terrified, she looked up into the liquid brown eyes of the loveliest quarter horse she had ever seen.

"Well, aren't you a beauty?" She laughed with relief. "Looks like I'll be able to borrow a horse after all. Now if I can just find a way to get myself on you without passing out... that will be the real trick."

Searching the ground, she found a fallen log not too far off. Using it, she hoisted herself up carefully and managed to seat herself without too much fuss. "Matt would be so disappointed to know you used a log," she said, shaking her head. "Well, I'd like to see him do the same with only one good arm." She was talking to herself again, a sure sign she was losing her mind. "He will just be happy for you to get home in one piece. So, let's go."

She was turning in the right direction when she noticed him. With the fighting mostly over, Eli had stopped to gather up Davey's body. His face, etched with sadness, was dirt-streaked, and despite the evening chill, he was drenched with sweat and no small amount of blood. She wanted nothing more than to run to him and wrap her arms around him.

"Leave it to me to want something I can't have," she mused. "God, Ry, you really are crazy."

Shaking her head, she prepared again to take her leave. She had not moved more than about two steps, however, when a snapping twig startled them both. The sound echoed loudly in the nearly silent night. Oh to be sure, there were still a few moans and groans coming from the field, but they were far enough away that this small corner seemed almost desolate. From the looks of it, there was a lone surviving raider who thought the same.

Eli turned sharply toward the sound, his vision obscured by the dense smoke. Even so, he reached for his rifle, ready to take the shot if needed. Unfortunately for him, he would never get the chance.

From her vantage point, Ry could see what he could not—the sniper had a clear shot at him and would not even need to move to take it. That he'd not already done so was due entirely to the acrid smoke that wafted in thick clouds across the ruined field. At any moment, the smoke would clear just long enough and he would make the kill.

"No way for him to miss from there, either," Ry whispered sadly. Her heart thudded painfully in her chest as she wrestled momentarily with her conscience.

"I have to…" She was sobbing quietly now, nearly tearing out what little was left of her hair at the agony of making such a heart-wrenching decision. Finally, sparing only one more brief thought of Matt and home, she kneed her horse into action. Battle-trained, it needed only the slightest bit of encouragement to respond instantly to her command. With Eli's life hanging in the balance, she raced back across the field toward the enemy.

At the last minute, sensing that his life was truly in danger the sniper changed targets, and Ry felt a sharp, searing pain as the bullet hit. Even so, she never slowed. Bearing down on the doomed man, she gripped the reins tighter and ran him into the ground.

Barely conscious from the pain, she slowly made her way back over to where Eli was standing.

"Are you completely insane?" he yelled, lowering his rifle as he finally recognized the rider coming toward him.

"Saving your arse again, I see." She tried for a grin, but her face didn't seem to be working quite right as the cool numbness invaded her body.

"Jesus, you're hurt." He reached out to touch the stain that was just beginning to seep through the front of her shirt.

"Eh, I'm good." She shrugged, trying desperately to ignore the throbbing pain in her chest. She was so close, especially now that she had a horse. If she could hang on just a bit longer, all would be fine. "Just need to get myself home. I'll be going now, if it's all the same to you."

She turned her horse, then stopped, and Eli watched, horrified, as she tumbled to the ground.

"Shit, shit... just hold on!"

He spared a quick glance toward the young boy whose body he'd been trying to collect and realized there was really no question in his mind about which one was more important. Saying a brief prayer over Davey and hoping that Cam or one of his other men would find the boy soon enough, he gently gathered Ry up in his arms and haphazardly managed to get them both back up on the quarter horse. He tied the reins of his own to the saddle so it could follow behind them.

"Just a little longer," he said again, mostly for his own benefit. His hands were shaking, and he clutched at the reins, looking desperately for anything resembling shelter. About to give up hope, he saw an abandoned slave shack and sighed in relief.

Set back in the trees, it wasn't much to look at, and in the darkness, he'd very nearly missed it. In truth, if not for the faint shimmer of firelight reflecting off the broken glass, he would have ridden right past it. The front walls were entirely burnt out, and the kudzu vines had long since taken over, but the back half seemed to be sturdy enough.

"Guess this will have to do." As he dismounted, he noticed that Ry's medical bag was tied to the saddle. *Well, at least something is going my way.* He grabbed it and carried Ry into the shack.

Though the floor was hard-packed dirt, the walls kept off the worst of the chill. The temperature was plummeting now that night had fallen, or at least it felt that way now that the battle rage was leaving him. Either way, they were going to need a small fire unless they wanted to freeze to death in the night. Running back outside, Eli pulled the bedrolls off the horses. Whomever the horse had been stolen from, at least they'd been well-prepared. Settling Ry down on the pallet, he covered her up, thankful to see the gentle rise and fall of her chest.

"Still breathing. That's a good sign. Now let's see about that fire."

Searching through the debris, he found enough stones to make a decent pit, and soon, the small blaze had the room pleasantly warm. Steeling himself for his next task, he took a swig of whiskey from the bottle he found in Ry's bag. "I think this more qualifies as medicinal purposes." He laughed, a slightly mad look in his eyes as he replaced the cap.

Turning to his patient, he pulled the covers back then slowly unbuttoned the blood-stained shirt. He noticed the swollen shoulder, and the bruise that was turning ugly shades of green and purple, but as it wasn't bleeding, he turned his attention elsewhere.

The bindings gave him pause, and he stared at them curiously as he ran his fingers over the material. Later, he would tell himself that it was probably one of the things that had saved her life—the fact that her chest had been bound so tightly, immediately staunching the flow of blood—but for now, it was just one more thing to add to the puzzle. Taking his knife, he ripped carefully through the linen strips then slowly pulled back the layers, trying not to disturb the clots that had already formed over the wound. The wound was located just above the creamy curve of her right breast.

"What the hell?" The knife slipped from his hand as it dawned on him exactly what he was looking at. "A woman… it makes perfect sense." He gasped, and suddenly, all the little things that had been slowly driving him crazy over the last couple of weeks fell into place. His relief, however welcome, was quickly replaced by anger—anger at the deception and anger that she had toyed so heartlessly with his emotions.

"But why?" He tried to get a hold of himself, at the very least long enough to finish treating her wounds.

He let his mind run over the events of the last several weeks as he carefully lifted Ry up. Her warm body rested gently against his as he removed the rest of her bindings, noting, again with relief, the exit wound in her back. "Well, at least I don't have to dig in there to find a bullet."

Still out cold, she gave no response, but it helped calm him to talk to her, even if she wasn't talking back. "Probably better, really," he whispered. "At this point, I'm not entirely sure that I'm all that ready to hear what you have to say for yourself." Still, his hands were gentle as he sewed her wounds and carefully bandaged them back up.

She was damn lucky, really. If she'd been hit even the slightest bit to the left, it would have hit bone, or worse, punctured a lung. As it was, it had passed right through the fleshy part. To be sure, she would certainly be sore for a while, but it wasn't nearly as bad as it could have been.

"Okay, you... I've got to go see about my men. Can't have them thinking I've deserted."

Dropping a quick kiss on her forehead, he covered her back up. Fairly certain that she wouldn't be waking up anytime soon, he made sure the fire was well-banked for the night then mounted up and headed back to the field.

After riding back to where Ry had so recently saved his life again, Eli was thankful to see that someone else had collected Davey's body. As for the rest, it didn't look as if anyone was coming to claim any of the enemy dead.

"Such a waste," he mused, running his hand across his face.

His head was beginning to ache from the smoke, and he truly hoped he wasn't going to have to ride all the way back to camp before he found what was left of the men under his command. Sighing, he picked his way across the field.

"Captain."

Eli turned at the sound, and it took him a moment to recognize his lieutenant. Cam's normally ginger hair was almost jet black, streaked with dirt and soot from the fire that still sputtered at the edges of the field.

"How many did we lose?" he asked, not even bothering to try to explain where he had been.

"Just the one." Cam's voice hitched slightly.

They had all been fond of Davey. He'd been so young but eager to please, and they had all spent a good deal of time training him hard. Willing that their guidance would be enough to keep him safe through the end of the war—clearly, it hadn't been. Shaking his head sadly, Cam pulled his thoughts back to the current situation. "About a handful of others are wounded, thankfully none too seriously, though. You were the only one we couldn't find, or we would have been halfway back to camp by now."

Eli nodded. "Yeah, sorry about that. Thought I saw some raiders taking off through the trees. Went out to make sure they weren't doubling back around." The lie came easy, too easy really, especially considering he had never needed to lie about anything before. He wasn't entirely sure he liked the feeling it left in the pit of his stomach. "If you all want to head back, I'm going to scout around a bit longer." He waved his hand vaguely toward the tree line. "We got lucky today. Don't want us to be caught unawares again."

Cam nodded as Eli went on. "Should be back sometime within the next day or so. You all stay out of sight and rest up best you can. Would be nice to find out where these boys have their hidey-hole. Then we can hit 'em hard and put an end to this mess." He tried to sound enthusiastic, but in truth, he just didn't have the stomach for it any longer.

Cam was a good man and a good soldier. Like Eli, he was originally from somewhere in the south, though his parents had moved the whole family up to New York sometime in his boyhood. Despite the change in geography, he still carried with him a distinctive southern drawl that he'd never quite been able to shake loose. He was reliable and loyal, almost to a fault, and was so used to following Eli's orders that he didn't even think twice before nodding in agreement.

"Yes Sir! Be careful out there. See you in a few days."

Feeling guilty for deceiving him, Eli watched as he rode off then turned back toward the shack and the woman he was likely throwing his career away for.

Ry was just as he had left her, her pale skin glowing in the faint light of the fire. There was a sheen of sweat on her brow, but thankfully, her skin was cool and only slightly clammy to the touch. "No sign of fever, at least," he said.

Then damning the rest of the world all to hell, he lay down beside her and wrapped her gently in his arms. "You better wake up in the morning," he whispered. "I may be in love with you, but if you don't give me a chance to kick your arse first, I'm going to be really angry."

Pressing a kiss to her lips, he let the exhaustion claim him.

CHAPTER NINE

Virginia: November 16, 1863

For the briefest of moments, Ry thought she was home again, warm and safe in her own bed, the events of the past week just a terrible nightmare. Shifting her body ever so slightly, she slowly opened her eyes to the late afternoon sun that was shining weakly through the cracked panes. In confusion, she tried to sit up, and the pain hit her. Raw and burning, it brought tears to her eyes, making her gasp out loud. The memories of the night before flashed rapidly before her eyes. Shaking, she took a deep breath and looked around, relief washing over her as she realized Eli was standing on the far side of the room.

"Cap'n…" Ry croaked, her voice hoarse with pain. "Captain." She said it again, somewhat louder this time, forcing the word out, as she tried to get his attention.

She saw him turn toward her and was instantly afraid. His eyes were like twin pools of liquid steel, and his jaw was clenched tight. Only in battle had she ever seen him like this, and certainly he had never directed such anger at her.

Oh God, he knows!

"Rylee James," Eli said with unexpected restraint. Any trace of the gentleness he'd had the night before had vanished. The long hours he had spent this morning putting all the pieces of the puzzle together had fairly ripped his heart in two. He was more than ready to take it out on the one responsible for it all. A brave woman risking her life for her country he could accept, even admire. But a spy… never!

"I've been going crazy this last week thinking I should have known you from somewhere. I racked my brain, thinking that if I could just pull that elusive detail out of the depths of my mind, I could rest easier." His voice was thick with days of suppressed frustration, barely held in check by what little was left of his self-control. "As it was, I might never have figured it out if not for your unfortunate little accident. Even seeing you with your brother didn't do the trick."

Pacing around the room, he shook his head, motioning her to silence when she opened her mouth to mumble some sort of meaningless protest.

"I bet you didn't know that I knew your brother, did you?" he continued. "No? Guess he wouldn't have mentioned it to you, and there had certainly been no reason for me to tell some doctor I'd just met that I knew one of the prisoners from before the war."

Eli walked closer to the pallet, and Ry did her best to shrink back under the covers, but even the slightest movements seemed to cause her pain. She searched desperately for any clues as to what his intentions were. If he had any mercy at all, he would kill her now and put a swift end to her misery.

Suddenly, he laughed, a sharp twisted little sound. "God, what a mess this is."

He stopped just out of her reach, and for a moment, she forgot to breathe. As little stars began to form in front of her eyes, instinct kicked in, and her straining lungs gasped for air. Still, he stood there watching her, and despite her fear, she willed herself to look him in the eye. Trembling slightly, it galled her that she was so afraid of him now. She thought back over the last several days and realized that more than anything, she didn't want him to hate her.

It was surprising, really. For weeks, her own hate had been the fuel that kept her going. This man had occupied her home, kept her brother prisoner, and even now held her own fate in the palm of his hand. Yet it was all she could do not to fling herself at his feet and beg for forgiveness. As horrible as it was, the physical pain in her body was nothing compared to the pain in her heart.

Oh God, I'm in love with him. She barely kept herself from blurting the words out loud, as her eyes widened in shock. Rubbing her hands over her face, she slowly gained control over her emotions. If all that she'd been through in the last few weeks had taught her nothing else, she knew that whatever was coming, she would at the very least stand up and take the news with whatever was left of her pride and dignity intact.

Carefully, she rose from the pallet, and though she nearly cried out loud from the pain, she finally managed to stand up straight. Shaking like a leaf, her knees ready to buckle at the slightest provocation, she closed her eyes to steady herself. Opening them again and gazing directly at Eli, she spoke.

"What are your intentions?"

Eli was truly at a loss, and his first instinct was to lash out in anger. Obviously, she was a spy, and it was his duty to see that she was taken into custody as soon as possible. But for once, his infallible sense of right and wrong was, well, failing. Ever since Ry had joined up with his command, he... no she—God, how could he reconcile that fact—had done nothing but earn the respect of not only himself but many of the other men in the camp that she had worked with. He had trusted her with his life—more than once, when it came down to it—and he now realized that trust had been a sham, a convenient ruse to save her precious brother.

"God, what a woman!" he murmured to himself. Anyone should be so lucky to have someone who loved them like that. He was torn between admiration and condemnation, but his protective instincts kicked in despite himself. *Her brother should be shot for leaving her behind to face the consequences.* Of course, he realized as well that if she hadn't gotten caught in the crossfire of this latest skirmish, she very likely would have succeeded with her plan to just slip away.

A woman. He still couldn't believe he hadn't known. Even now with the traces of blood, dirt, and gunpowder streaked across her face, he was having trouble picturing her as the man he had known. He shuddered inwardly as he remembered the exact moment he had discovered her secret. He could never let her know that it had nearly unmanned him—seeing her covered in all that blood and realizing there was a female body underneath it all. He must have been blind not to have seen the truth.

Ry was in agony, and she was beginning to regret her decision to stand up and *take it like a man.* Eli was just staring at her, as if she had somehow sprouted wings. He was obviously doing everything in his power to torture her mentally and physically, and frankly, she was tired of it. The longer he stood there, the angrier she became. Finally, she snapped.

"Say something, damn it!" she yelled, her voice echoing in the otherwise silent room.

Eli was in shock. She was mad at him? "What the hell is wrong with you?" he asked, grabbing her uninjured arm.

Long past being afraid, she only knew that she had to get away from him. She couldn't stand for him to look at her that way; it was simply more than she could bear. Struggling, despite the searing pain in her breast, she tried to pull away from him, but his hand was vise-like around her arm.

152

"Let me go!" she demanded.

"Or what?" Eli pulled her closer, his gaze boring into hers.

Ry froze. She felt faint again and briefly wondered if it was from the loss of blood or if it was simply his presence that was making her feel that way.

For his part, Eli was barely able to restrain himself. Clenching his fists, he wanted to throttle her, and in his mind's eye, he could see his hands wrapping around her perfect, slim neck and slowly squeezing. Reaching out, his free hand moved over her shoulder, and her green eyes grew wide.

Such beautiful eyes, he realized. Staring into them was like getting lost in a summer forest. The dappled shades of green gave way to darker mysterious pools. It would be so easy to sink into their depths.

Ry's whole body was on fire, and it wasn't just the pain of her wounds, though that was there as well. She knew she had to say something, anything to get him away from her so she could regain her sanity. Its shredded edges slipped further and further away between the physical trauma of the last few days and Eli's seemingly careless indecision regarding her very life. If she didn't act now, her mind would surely shatter into nothingness.

A small sound escaped her lips, and for a moment, Eli regained his senses… but only for a moment. Ry's mouth had gone dry, and unaware of the devastating effect it would have on him, she slowly flicked out her tongue to wet her lips.

His grip on her shoulder tightened painfully, and instantly, she knew she'd made a terrible mistake. Eyes going dark with naked desire, he leaned in, and before she could utter a word of protest, he kissed her.

The world was melting; there could be no other explanation. Ry's rational mind screamed at her to break free from him, but in the end, her body betrayed her, and she leaned in closer to him, grabbing onto him for support as she felt her knees weaken.

Eli knew he needed to stop the madness that was occurring, but his mind seemed to have completely shut down. He felt Ry move closer to him, her warm curves fitting his body perfectly. As he continued to assault her mouth, he ran his hands down her back, caressing her. Gently, he pulled her hips toward him, but a soft cry of pain brought him up short.

"Damn it!" He suddenly remembered that she was injured and cursed himself for adding to her distress. Ry just stared at him, dazed and trembling, and he started to move away. "I don't want to hurt you," he said quietly, his expression unreadable.

She knew that once they were back in the real world, she would likely go to prison as a spy and just as likely never see him again. She also knew that if she could have just this one perfect moment with him, she would have the strength to face whatever fate had in store for her. Knowing this, she didn't hesitate. For now, she pushed aside all the remaining fears and doubts that crowded her mind. Carefully, she unbuttoned her shirt and dropped it to the floor. Then she stepped out of her pants.

Eli looked her up and down, his heart thudding painfully in his chest. The sight of her took his very breath away. She was perfectly exquisite, and again, he was amazed that he could have lived with her day in and day out without realizing that she was a woman.

He reached out and drew her to him, suddenly afraid. The bandages and the bruising on her shoulders were a sharp contrast to the smooth creaminess of her skin, and more than anything else at this moment, he didn't want to cause her any more pain. With infinite gentleness, he began to kiss her, slowly making his way down her body, intent on kissing every hurt away.

Her body arched toward him as his hands caressed her, touching her in places that made her whole body tingle with pleasure. With great care, he laid her back on the pallet. "You are so beautiful," he whispered, his voice hoarse with desire.

With every touch and every taste, Ry felt as if she was flying. Nothing in her life had prepared her for the multitude of sensations that were flooding her body.

Eli stood before her and quickly removed his clothes. He was so hard that it was almost painful. He honestly couldn't remember the last time, if ever, he had wanted a woman as much as he wanted the one that was lying spread out before him. She was a veritable feast, just waiting for him to partake.

"Are you sure?" he asked as he knelt before her.

With a care for her injury, she pulled him into her embrace. "Yes."

He kissed her mouth as he entered her. She was tight, but her body was more than willing, and she stretched accommodatingly, her delicious warmth closing over him.

There was a slight pain, but she held him close, and soon it passed. Slowly, they moved, their bodies in tune with one another. Sensation after sweet

157

sensation built, one on top of the other, and just when Ry thought she couldn't possibly fly any higher, he sent her soaring far beyond what she'd ever imagined.

Stunned and near insensible by the sheer intensity of it all, they both lay unmoving as the spasms slowly subsided. When Eli shifted slightly, Ry made a sound of protest.

"Shhh… I don't want my weight to hurt you." He moved so that she was wrapped more comfortably in his arms. He kissed her lightly on the lips, and she snuggled closer.

Though it had been more than worth the discomfort to her injuries, her exertions had taken their toll, and she whimpered softly as she drifted off to sleep.

Eli continued to watch her. Exhaustion was his constant companion these last few days, but still, sleep eluded him. *I should have never allowed this to happen.* The thought came unbidden as feelings of guilt and regret surged up within him.

His duty to his country was clear, but what of his duty to himself and his own heart? Knowing the consequences, he just wasn't sure he would be able to let her go when the time came. He would have to harden himself. This could change nothing.

CHAPTER TEN

Virginia: November 17, 1863

"This was a mistake."

Of course, Eli wasn't crass enough to say the words out loud, but Ry could see it plainly in his face, in the very way he held his body. And though she knew it for truth, it didn't make the pain of rejection any less intense.

"So... where do we go from here?" She wanted to get the inevitable over with.

It was admirable, the way she didn't shy away from it. That she didn't beg or try to use whatever it was that was between them as a bargaining chip for her freedom. Eli kept his tone as level as possible under the circumstances. "We'll take it slow, but we need to head back to camp as soon as you're ready. Would be a good idea as well for you to maintain your disguise for now rather than make any drastic changes.

There will be time enough for that later when we meet up with General Meade."

She nodded, feeling that there was no real need for words at this point. Not that she had much else to say to him, anyway.

"You know I don't have a choice." He said it softly, almost begging her to understand the position he was in. "Once they're sure that you don't pose any sort of threat, they'll likely just send you back home. But for now, you know too much."

It was a ridiculous statement, given that she really didn't know anything of the sort, but as there was really nothing she could say that would make any difference, she started getting dressed. Her movements were slow, and to be honest, she hadn't the slightest idea how she was going to sit on a horse with her right arm mostly out of commission. As it was, she couldn't even dress herself without wanting to scream.

Sensing her distress, Eli reached out and finished wrapping her bindings then helped her button her shirt. For the briefest of moments, she thought he was going to kiss her again, but the moment passed, and he simply turned away to start packing up their gear.

"You can ride with me until we get a bit closer to camp," he said. "Even if anyone sees, it's clear you're injured, so they won't think too much of it."

"Good to know you've a plan for everything," she retorted, biting her lip to keep from fully losing her temper.

He didn't give her the satisfaction of a reply, and only the momentary darkening of his eyes gave her any indication that he'd even heard her. Heartsick and weary, she took a last look around the shack then grabbed her medical bag and headed for the door. "Ready when you are."

The ride back was nothing short of torture, even though it was relatively uneventful. In a perfect world, they might have been two lovers, riding together, enjoying the last blaze of glory from the fall foliage. In the real world, he was taking her back to hell. If she'd had the strength to fight, she would have, but she wouldn't have gotten very far, even if she'd had it in her to stab him right there and then.

"How much longer will we be in camp?" she asked, looking for anything to end the silence that had stretched on for miles.

"Only a day or so," he replied curtly, not offering up any other information.

She stifled a sigh and continued on, undeterred. "Okay... different topic. What do you do when you aren't at war?"

At first, she thought he wasn't going to say anything, and as the minutes stretched on, she resigned herself to enduring more of the silent treatment he was so good at giving.

"Dunno..." he finally answered. "Been at war for so long, I think I've forgotten what it is that normal people do."

The ire that had been slowly building within her melted away. For such a casual reply, that one sentence spoke volumes. She could hear, in the very sound of his voice, just how sick and tired of it all he really was. Linking her fingers through his, she squeezed gently. "Hopefully soon, we'll all get to find out."

"Yeah... maybe."

He lapsed into silence again, lost somewhere in his own private hell. Giving up on conversation, Ry leaned back and closed her eyes, trusting that Eli would keep her from falling while she dozed.

About an hour from camp, Ry switched to her own mount. It was a painstaking process, and she was pale and shaking by the time she was properly seated. Worried, Eli kept himself within arm's reach, ready to catch her if the pain proved too much.

"Just let me do the talking when we get back to my men," he said as they rode out. "They probably won't question it much since you were with us before, but I don't really want to make things any more difficult than they need to be."

"Makes sense," she replied. Not like she could really complain since *more difficult* would likely include her being chained, or worse, beaten like the poor soldier she had tended on her first night in camp.

He must have seen the fear in her eyes. "I've sent those bastards on, but still, the men I'm with trusted you. They won't take it kindly when they learn the truth. It will be bad enough that I'm not telling them immediately."

Not waiting for a reply, he kneed his mount, leaving her to struggle along as they hurried the last few miles, eager to make camp before sunset.

"Captain!" Cam saluted as they rode in. "Good to have you back."

Eli nodded. "Hope you're all well-rested," he said. "Need to go ahead and pack up as much as we can tonight. We'll be riding out at first light. Area is clear enough for now. We need to get on out of here and meet up with General Meade."

He could see them eyeing Ry, but as he expected, not one of them said anything. They would continue to accept her as they had before, at least until someone told them differently. For her part, Ry tried her best to be unobtrusive. As it was, she could barely stand. Sensing that she was at her limit, Eli motioned her into what had previously been the officer's quarters.

Since the main force had moved out, those remaining had consolidated their gear and hadn't seen any reason to waste the four good walls the building provided.

"Much better than sleeping on the ground, out in the cold," they had all agreed.

Ry stumbled toward the door, grasping at the frame to keep herself upright. Eli stepped in behind her, holding out an arm to steady her. "There's a spare bunk in the back corner. You can use that for the night."

She looked around as she walked toward it, noting that it was also conveniently placed so that if she tried to escape, she would have to pass not only Eli, but pretty much everyone else who would be sleeping in the small room.

"Thanks," she murmured. Without any further thought, she laid out her blankets and fell promptly to sleep.

CHAPTER ELEVEN

Virginia: November 18, 1863

Eli hadn't been kidding. There was barely a sliver of dawn breaking when they moved out. It might have been beautiful under other circumstances. The frost-tipped grass sparkled in the pale light, crunching softly as they rode out of camp. Again, he was riding so close to her, they might as well have been on the same horse. Having slept straight through the night, Ry felt a little better, but still the strain of riding was taking its toll.

As the miles passed, she prayed desperately that they wouldn't be attacked. The very thought of having to do more than let her horse lead the way was nearly enough to send her into a panic. Even though it might have given her the opportunity to escape, she had a feeling she wouldn't get far in the shape she was in.

They rode in silence. Not that they really expected any surprises, but just in case, there was no sense asking for trouble. Even to Ry, who had almost been born in the saddle, the pace was grueling, but she knew better than to complain. As it was, she was terrified about what would happen to her once they met up with the rest of Meade's army. She had tried to explain to Eli that she hadn't paid attention to much of anything except getting her brother out, but he'd refused to listen. And if he didn't believe her, how would she convince anyone else that she really wasn't a spy?

God, what if they want to hang me? The words tumbled through her mind before she could stop them, and she thought for a moment that she was going to be sick. That feeling only got worse, the closer they got to their destination. Her hands were shaking so hard, she could barely hold on to the reins.

"I don't think I can do this," she finally whispered when they stopped to water the horses.

"Huh?" Eli asked, perplexed.

169

"You want me to just ride in and hand myself over to people who don't even know me, people who could very well do to me what those men did to that boy," she said, reminding him of the horrors she witnessed her first night in camp. "How exactly do you expect me to do this?"

He turned and looked at her. "What do you want me to do? Let you go?" His eyes blazed with anger, which quickly turned to anguish. "You know I can't do that."

There was genuine regret in his gaze, and she knew if it had just been his life at stake, he likely would have taken her straight to her own door himself.

Deflated, the fight went out of her. "I know," she said soothingly. "But that doesn't mean I have to go gracefully."

She wanted nothing more than for him to hold her and tell her that everything was going to work out for the best. But she was a big girl, and she had known all along that there could be consequences for her actions. Now it was time to face them. Struggling to keep the tears from falling, she walked away. She thought he might call after her and warn her to stick close, but then she realized what he already knew; it wasn't as if she had anywhere else to go.

Cam eased over to where Eli was checking his horse's hooves. "Something you want to tell me?"

"About what?"

"I hadn't noticed before, probably because I spent quite a bit of time out scouting and she spent most of her time in with the prisoners or avoiding the rest of us, but…"

Eli went still. He'd heard Cam loud and clear… *she* not *he*. "How long have you known?" he asked.

"Well, I still might not have, but part of it was the way you were hovering. Also, I finally got a good look at the way she walks." He grinned wickedly. "How the hell did any of us miss that walk?"

171

"She was probably doing a better job of hiding it before." Eli shook his head, fighting the primitive urge to growl in protest that another man would even look at Ry. "She was injured pretty good the other night, and it's taking up a lot of her concentration at the moment."

"How involved was she in that mess we rode into?" Cam looked at him closely, and to his credit, Eli had the grace to look guilty.

"The raiders? Not at all." He replied instantly, making it abundantly clear that whatever else she may have done, she had never purposefully put any of them in danger through her actions. "Her bad luck to be crossing the same field we were, at the wrong time. Can't say I'm not glad that she was, though, or I wouldn't be here to talk about it." Eli shivered, remembering how close a call it had really been for him. "Unfortunately, she was responsible for our prisoner—her brother—getting loose. So as you can see, I couldn't just let her go."

Cam nodded. "Makes sense, I guess. But do you really think they'll treat her well when you turn her over?"

"Dunno. I'd like to think I can keep her safe, keep her in a cell long enough that whatever she might have overheard while she was with us would be useless, but I'm starting to worry that it won't be enough."

Cam shook his head. "Might work as long as you're in camp. But if you ride out for more than a day or so, I wouldn't count on someone not taking advantage. Really, who's going to stop them? You know how they get about spies, and half of them haven't seen a woman in months. It would be too much to resist…" He left the thought hanging.

"What else is there to do? If I let her go, I'm betraying my country and putting everyone's lives at risk." Eli was nearly beside himself. The words Cam spoke were the very words that had run through his own mind a million times in the last couple of days. Jumbled together, they were nearly driving him mad.

"Do you really think she would do that?" Cam asked him pointedly.

"No, I don't, and clearly you don't. But *they* don't know that, and it's their thoughts on the subject that count the most. If anyone else found out…" He paused, fighting for the sense of calm that normally surrounded him. "If they found out, I would be shot for treason."

Eli looked utterly defeated. He knew Cam was dead right. Hell, even Ry had already called him on it. "If you have another suggestion, I'm all for it," he said in desperation.

They stood staring at her for several long minutes before Cam finally replied. "Might be that I do," he said a bit cryptically. "Just how much do you care about keeping her safe?"

Eli should have seen it coming. Cam had been more than observant about everything else; it was one of the reasons why he was Eli's second in command in the first place. But still, he felt a little blindsided by the question.

174

"What do you have in mind, exactly?" he asked warily.

Cam shifted his weight from one foot to the other. "Well, if she was your wife, for example, rather than just some random spy, they might take a little better care of her. Don't ya think?"

His heart lurched painfully in his chest. It made perfect sense, of course, but oh, how God was laughing at him. She probably hated him for everything he had put her through in the last couple of days—hell, the last couple of weeks—and now he was going to have to propose and somehow get her to accept. Turning it carefully over in his mind, he could see no other viable options. He knew this was really the only way, short of just letting her go.

He looked at Cam and nodded slowly in agreement. "Don't suppose you know where we can find a church anywhere around here?"

"Might just be that I do," Cam said with a grin.

Predictably, Ry laughed in his face.

To be fair, his proposal had been lacking in the charm and romance department, but given the seriousness of the situation, he had felt that a straightforward approach was more appropriate.

"Did you want me to get down on my knee?" he asked, glaring at her. "I'm willing to do this to protect you. You should be grateful."

"Grateful?" she spat. Her eyes narrowed to tiny emerald pinpricks, and if he hadn't jumped back out of her reach, he was quite sure she would have probably clawed his face off. "If you'd just let me go—"

Interrupting her, he grabbed her arm, still trying to keep the rest of his body out of harm's way. "We've been over that. You know I can't." Taking a chance, he leaned in close, trailing a finger down her face. "If we had any other choice, I would take it; you know that. But given your fears, this is the only thing we could come up with."

"Who's we?"

"Cam noticed something was amiss—lucky for you. He agrees that turning you over without any sort of additional protection is foolhardy at best."

She glanced over at Eli's lieutenant, and he smiled lazily, nodding back at her.

"Ugh, men!" she said, exasperated.

"Is that a 'yes'?" Eli asked, grinning.

"The only one you are ever going to get," she replied testily.

In truth, there was some small part of her that was thrilled at the idea of being his wife, but considering the circumstances, it was just too much for her to deal with all at once. Still, if it meant keeping her neck out of a noose, she was pretty much willing to do just about anything at this point.

"Let's get this over with."

The church was on the way—a charming little stone affair with simple but lovely stained glass to let in the light. The ceremony only took a few short minutes, and they had to make a modest donation to the priest, then the two of them were officially man and wife. Proud of the way they'd both managed to say their vows without stumbling too badly over the words, Eli had lingered over the "kissing the bride" part.

"Might as well get some enjoyment out of this day," he'd whispered to Ry, before taking a few extra moments to savor the taste of her lips.

Thankfully, she hadn't seemed to mind. Part of him wondered if she would stick with him after the war or if this was just simply another way of getting what she wanted.

They'd fashioned a ring of sorts out of some leftover scraps of metal, and though it was the best they could do for now, he wished he'd had his grandmother's heirloom ring with him. Safe in his dresser at home, the simple diamond band had come to him after her death, and he dreamed now of seeing it on Ry's slim finger. His grandmother would have loved Ry. A fiery woman in her own right, his grandmother had always kept his grandfather on his toes—one of the few people who ever could. He hoped one day that he would have the chance to tell Ry all about her.

As a wedding present, Cam had explained the detour to the rest of the men. Eli still didn't know what sort of story he had concocted, but it must have been a good one, because no one had even blinked at the delay. The thought of stopping and making camp had crossed his mind, more than once in fact—anything to delay the inevitable. But at this point, they were so close to their destination, there was no way to plausibly explain stopping for the night. At least not without some sort of serious reason for doing so. The area was safe enough, but in truth, every minute they delayed put their lives at risk. He just wasn't willing to take any more chances with their safety.

"All right, let's get moving," he said finally.

"Just a minute." Ry signaled to him then leaned in close and whispered with a blush, "Nature calls."

Eli made a little sound of annoyance but nodded. "Hurry up. We've wasted too much time here already."

"Gee, what a romantic way to refer to your wedding day," he heard her say as she walked into the brush for a quick moment of privacy.

"What's the hold up?" Cam asked. The quick moment had turned into several minutes, and the men were starting to get a bit antsy.

"Not sure; I'll go check." Eli headed toward the path Ry had taken. Past the tree line, there was sparse cover and only a few places that could conceal a person. But after a brief search, it was clear that she was nowhere to be found. "What the hell?" he asked, looking around in consternation.

"What's wrong?" Cam asked, joining him.

Eli gave him a terse reply. "She's gone!"

"What do you mean gone?" Cam asked. "There's nowhere for her to go, and all her gear is back with her horse. Only a fool would take off in this weather, especially with night coming on, not to mention her injuries. She didn't strike me as a fool."

"Well, she's not here. You're welcome to look for yourself," Eli said, as Cam made his way around the clearing. "This just doesn't make any sense," he continued, shaking his head. "Why go through with the ceremony if she was just going to take off?" He was angry to be sure, but underneath it all was hurt that she had actually left him, that she didn't trust him enough to keep her safe.

"Dunno," Cam said, just as confused. "But the real question now is what are we going to do about it?"

"Do we go after her, you mean?" Eli asked. "Honestly, I'm so tired of this shit, I'm tempted just to let her go and wash my hands of it all."

"Might be for the best," Cam agreed. "Not like we can really afford to stop and go after her. You

181

probably noticed, but there are no signs of a struggle, so whatever she did, she did it on her own."

"Yeah, I noticed."

Eli's shoulders sagged in defeat, and he took a long last look around for any small bit of evidence that they might have missed. Other than their own prints, even the hard-packed dirt looked undisturbed, as if they had been the only ones to pass this way. Nothing moved, and the woods were as silent and still as the grave.

He resigned himself to the fact that she was truly gone. "Don't see that we have much choice. We can't keep delaying our return."

"Let's go, then." Cam started back to where their men were waiting. "If anyone asks, we can just say that the she got an urgent message regarding some sort of emergency back home. Not like anyone can prove different."

Eli nodded then glanced around for a final time. "You better stay far away from me, Rylee James.

I've made enough stupid decisions in the last week because of you. Don't make me regret this one too."

If looks could kill, her brother would have been nothing more than a desiccated shell of a man. He must have been smarter than he looked, though, because once the woods were clear of any other human presence, he released the iron-hard grip he had been keeping on her mouth and jumped back just out of her reach.

"What the hell do you think you're doing?" she nearly screamed at him.

"Um… thought it was pretty clear that I was rescuing you." His puzzled look was endearing, and she was truly grateful not to be going to prison as a spy. But still, she had seen the look on Eli's face, heard the pain in his voice, and it was nearly killing her.

"If you would settle down, I've got a couple of horses not too far from here. We need to hurry if we're going to get to them before dark."

She followed along silently, her mouth opening several times to try to explain why she needed to go back, but the words just wouldn't come. No matter what she did, there was no winning. If she went back, odds were that being Eli's wife wouldn't be enough to save her, and at this point, it was clear that he was already feeling less than friendly toward her. Like as not, he probably wouldn't even care if she disappeared out of his life forever.

"Ry." Matt had stopped walking, and lost in thought, Ry tumbled right into him. "You okay?"

"Fine," she said distractedly. "Just wasn't paying attention is all. How did you find us, anyway? Thought I told you to go home and stay there."

"Yeah, right, like I was going to just leave you." Matt rolled his eyes at her. "Seriously, though, I did make it home you know—in record time, even. But when you didn't show up soon after, I knew something was wrong. Got word that they'd moved everyone up this way when I made contact with my superiors, so I was heading up to check things out. Pure luck that I came across you all when I did. When I saw the men getting ready to ride out again, I figured this would be my best chance of getting you. Would have been a much bigger risk trying to grab you later on, once you'd joined up with Meade."

She couldn't fault his logic, but she still hated for Eli to think that she had just run off. She might have taken the opportunity to do so on her own if she'd had the option, but now that the decision had been taken from her, she would just have to make the best of it.

Matt stopped suddenly again. And again, she stumbled into him, her mind miles away from the trail in front of her. This time, though, when he put his arm out to steady her, she cried out in pain.

"What is wrong with you?" This time, his look of concern was her undoing. Tears, wet and hot, streaked down her face. "Shit, don't cry," he begged.

But nonetheless, he held her close until she had cried herself out, leaving only a hollowed-out space where her heart used to be.

When the worst was over, Matt pulled out a ragged handkerchief and handed it to her.

Dabbing at her tears, Ry hiccupped once then smiled. "Can't believe you still have this." She'd hand-stitched it herself back in the days when Katie had still held out hope that she might be handy with a sewing needle. Soon after, it had become abundantly clear that sewing wasn't her calling, and they'd moved on to other lessons. Though to this day, it confounded them all how she could stitch up a wound perfectly yet fail so miserably at embroidery. Still, the handkerchief had been one of her better efforts, and she'd given it to Matt for Christmas the year before he'd left for West Point. The crude monogram had lost a few stitches, but it touched her that he'd held on to it.

"Seriously, Ry, what is going on?" he asked, refusing to let her change the subject.

"Just the stress of it all, I think. Being an adult is the worst." She tried for a laugh but settled for another hiccup as she finished drying the tears from her cheeks.

"Yeah, but that doesn't explain the yelp of pain when I touched you," he said pointedly.

She squirmed a bit at the direct look he gave her then decided on the truth, or at least part of the truth. "You know, I did almost make it home as well. Got out with no troubles at all; no one seemed to suspect a thing. Well, they might have wondered, but they had more important things on their minds. Unfortunately, some of your lot decided to unleash hell on the field I was crossing, though—on account of the Union boys who just happened to be passing by around the same time. Needless to say, talk about being in the wrong place at the wrong time."

"How bad were you hurt?" He asked it slowly, his normally sparkling green eyes turning to angry wave-tossed seas.

"All things considered, could have been a lot worse," she hedged. "And if it makes you feel any better, I rode the bastard down that did it." She was trying to soothe him, but it wasn't working.

"How bad?" he asked again, a hint of steel in his voice. No hope for holding off the inevitable storm that was coming.

"I was shot… just above my right breast. Got lucky. It went straight through without hitting any bone, but it still hurts like crazy when I move wrong. Eli tended it well enough, though, but—" She stopped as his eyes narrowed. "What?"

"Eli, is it?" he asked, his voice deceptively calm.

"Captain Webb," she replied, not quite understanding what the problem was. "He said you knew him."

"Just because I may have gone to West Point with the bastard, I don't see where it gives you the right to address him so familiarly," he said rather primly.

188

Ry bit her tongue but couldn't quite contain the laughter. "Good grief! Really? Next time, I'll be sure to tell him that my brother thinks my modesty is more important than my life. Honestly, I can't believe you're getting so worked up over this."

"There won't be a next time," he said. "Seriously, Ry, I'm getting you as far away from this mess as I can and then keeping you there, even if I have to tie you down."

"Stay out of trouble, and maybe I'll listen." She smiled, but his eyes held hers until she was forced to give in. With nothing left to say to each other, they continued on their way.

Daylight was fading when they finally reached the horses. The days were short enough this time of year, but within the confines of the densely packed pines, each hour was that much more precious.

"Let's ride out a bit further from here, then we can set up camp. Don't think anyone was following, but can't hurt to be cautious just in case."

Bone weary, Ry only nodded. Then with Matt's assistance, she mounted up and followed him deeper into the woods.

It was very nearly dark when they stopped. For sure, Ry could barely see her hands in front of her face as she slid carefully off her horse.

"I'll get a small fire going," Matt said. "Then we can have a bite to eat. Nothing to write home about, but there are some extra rations in my pack if you want to grab them."

"Of course," she said, watching as the small spark blazed to life, chasing away the darkness. Now that she could see where she was going, she made her way over to the packs, grabbing the food along with the canteen and a small pot to cook it all in.

While Matt took care of the grub, she went back and grabbed their bedrolls then set them up as close to the fire as she dared.

"Gonna be another cold one," she said.

"Looks like it," he replied. "Don't worry, though, I'll make sure to keep the fire going."

"I can help keep watch if you need me to," Ry offered.

"Nah, you get some rest. You look like you're about to fall over on your face."

"Gee, thanks. I love you too." Sticking her tongue out at him, she sat down next to the fire and wrapped her blankets around her. The smell of food was making her mouth water, and her stomach growled in anticipation.

"Keep stirring that for me, will you?" Matt asked. "I'm going to go take care of the horses." Not waiting for a reply, he walked off into the shadows. When he returned, they ate, and never one to be shy about food, Ry nearly licked her plate clean.

Matt laughed. "Hungry, were you?"

She grinned. "Maybe. Thanks."

The flames were hypnotic, and now that her belly was full, Ry could barely keep her eyes open.

"Go to sleep," Matt told her. "I'll keep an eye on things. You need your rest."

She nodded and was asleep before her head touched the ground. Sometime later, her eyes flew open as she felt Matt's hand gently touch her shoulder. Crouched down low beside her, he put a finger to his lips. On full alert, she listened intently. The fire that was helping to keep them alive through the night was now putting them at a serious disadvantage if there was anyone out there. Not only was it a shining beacon, but it made it hard to see into the darkness beyond. Though Matt had shielded it fairly well, Ry moved carefully to dampen it down completely. Being warm was all fine and good, but not at the expense of their lives.

Off to their left, she could hear someone moving around, and there was a muffled curse as a twig snapped loudly in the cold silence of the night. Barely daring to breathe, they waited, huddled together for warmth, hoping and praying that whoever was out there didn't accidentally stumble upon their campsite. It was nearly dawn before Matt felt that it was safe enough for them to build up the fire again.

"We'll eat quick, then let's get out of here. That was way too close."

CHAPTER TWELVE

Virginia: November 19 - 26, 1863

They made good time, stopping only once to dodge another Union patrol that was passing through. Once the way was clear, they remounted, and the rest of the trip was, to Ry's everlasting relief, uneventful.

"Smells like snow," she said as they rode down the lane to the house. "Good thing we're home. Wouldn't want to be out in that when it hits."

Matt sniffed the air and nodded. "Weather can do what it wants. I think I'm just going to hibernate."

"Will you be able to stay home for a while?" Ry asked.

"Think so. Officially, I'm still recovering from my injuries, which they were nice enough to let me do here at home since it's a lot closer than the nearest field hospital. So, I've got at least a little more time to stick around." He grinned. "Long enough to keep you from getting into more trouble at any rate."

She laughed, shaking her head. "Yeah, as if I'm the one who needs help keeping out of trouble."

Home. Just the sight of it brought tears to her eyes. "Wow. Didn't realize how much I missed being here." She eased herself off her horse. "Katie!" she yelled. "We're home."

"Oh, thank God!" Katie ran down the stairs, flung her arms around Ry, and hugged her tight. "Don't you even think about leaving again, you hear me?"

"Yes, ma'am!" Ry winced slightly, but she endured the pain, just happy to be safe at home.

"Get yourself upstairs." Katie shooed her. "I'll have Samuel bring hot water for a bath."

"Thanks, Katie." Ry made her way up the stairs to her room, and soon enough, she was relaxing in the warm water, taking care not to get her bandages wet.

"See you managed to get yourself banged up there," Katie said, adding a splash more hot water to the tub.

"It will heal up soon enough," Ry said with a shrug.

"Hmm... it better."

The water was turning cold when Ry finally stepped from the tub. Wrapping the linen towel around her body, she sat at the vanity and carefully removed her bandages. "Gonna have a beauty of a scar there," she said to herself, running her fingers over the jagged pink wound.

The stitches were holding well enough, but still, the injury wasn't very pretty to look at. "No infection, though, and that's definitely a good sign." Once she had changed her bandages, she made her way over to the bed. Wrapped in the warmth of her blankets, she was asleep within moments.

Near sunset, Katie brought her a tray of food, but Ry didn't even budge. "Well, it will be here on the table when you wake up," Katie whispered, not wanting to disturb her slumber.

It was still sitting there in the morning when Ry finally opened her eyes, sunlight streaming in. Getting up, she looked outside and saw the fresh, glistening snow blanketing the ground. She grinned. "Ha, nose hasn't failed me yet."

Ravenous, she picked at the tray of food. When it was gone, her belly rumbled in protest. "Well, that just won't do." Throwing her old woolen dress on, she went off to the kitchens in search of more.

"Good to see you up and about, Miss Ry," Katie said with a smile. "Think Matt's going to sleep the whole day away."

"Wouldn't blame him, honestly," Ry answered. "He didn't sleep much the last couple of days. Too busy keeping watch. I'd just let him be for now. He promised he was going to sleep for a week. Guess he's making good on it." She rummaged through the pantry, unable to make up her mind.

Finally, Katie shooed her out. "Go sit yourself down, and I'll cook you up a real meal. After everything you've been through, you should be resting, anyway."

"Yes, ma'am," Ry replied meekly. Though she had felt well-rested when she had gotten up, she was already starting to feel tired again. "I know better than to try arguing with you."

She hugged Katie then poured herself a cup of tea and sat at the kitchen table. Opening the tin in front of her, she found biscuits and happily nibbled at one, while Katie moved efficiently to make her breakfast. The resulting meal was nothing short of a feast.

She marveled at the eggs and strips of ham. "Katie, it's too much!"

"Well, those awful soldiers didn't take everything, and I've been saving up for when you got back. Now hush up and enjoy."

Ry was unable to hold back the tears that were welling up. "Thank you."

"Now, now… none of that." Katie patted her good shoulder. "Just glad the two of you are home safe; that's all that matters."

"Me too," Ry said. "Me too."

After the excitement of the last couple of weeks, being home was… well, she hated to say it— *boring*. Not that she missed the fear of being caught or being shot at, or the people dying around her, or really any of the long list of other things that had kept her constantly on edge. But still, there wasn't much to do at home—just sit and rest, then sit some more. Spending time with Matt was a wonderful gift, but with both their injuries still healing, they couldn't go out riding like they normally did. Not to mention, it probably wasn't all that safe for them to do so, anyway, even if they'd been in perfect health. So, as usually happens in such circumstances, it was only a matter of days before they felt the walls starting to close in.

They'd been picking at each other again. "Maybe I should head back to my unit," Matt finally said. Even though his wounds were still twinging a bit, having to endure another week or more of inactivity was likely to kill him, if Ry didn't do it first.

"What? No! You said you had time," Ry exclaimed, distressed at the thought of him leaving. "Figured you'd spend the holidays here then go back."

"Well, originally I'd thought about it, and it's true that I've been given home leave for at least another week or so to recover." He grinned. "Honestly, though, I'm just not sure the two of us will make it that long all cooped up in here together."

"They always say doctors make the worst patients. I'm sorry. I'll try to do better. Just don't leave yet," she begged.

"Fine, I'll at least stay through this day of Thanksgiving that Lincoln has decreed. The president and I may be on different sides of this godforsaken war, but the idea is sound. It never hurts to give thanks for the good things we still have. Besides, Katie would probably skin my hide if I left out of here before then, anyway. She's already been cooking like crazy. I never know how she manages to make what little we have stretch so far."

"She amazing. That's how," Ry said. "I should probably go see if there's anything I can do to help. For some reason, she keeps kicking me out."

"That's because your cooking… um… well…" Matt caught the murderous glint in Ry's eyes and prudently changed directions. "I'm sure Katie would love some help."

Rolling her eyes, Ry headed into the kitchen.

She stopped short at the door, staring at Katie's handiwork. "How in the world do you expect the four of us to eat all that?" Every available surface was covered with a dish of some sort—pies, late fall vegetables, casseroles, everything imaginable—and the smells were divine.

"It just looks like a lot, but really, it's only a bit of each thing." Katie smiled. "Besides, I know you and Matt have appetites that are more than up to the challenge."

Ry laughed. "You are going to make us fat. Can I help you with anything?"

"Being stuck in the house driving you that crazy, is it?" Katie asked.

"I know I should be grateful that we're both home safe, but between the cold and not knowing if there's anyone out there looking for me, being stuck inside is almost more than I can handle." She sighed and stole a bite of breaded stuffing from one of the pans.

"I know it's hard, but you'll do what you've always done... endure." Katie wrapped her arms around Ry and planted a kiss on her head.

Ry was silent for a few moments then simply nodded.

With one problem solved for the day, Katie turned back to the chaos in the kitchen. "Anyways, most everything is ready for the feast, but you could help me cover up those dishes over there. Then while I finish up a few things in here, you could set out the fine china so that the table is all ready for tomorrow."

"On my way!" Ry said.

"I don't think I can possibly eat another bite." Ry groaned, pressing her hand to her belly. "It was really wonderful, Katie. Thank you."

Katie nodded. "You are very welcome."

"I could definitely learn to enjoy celebrating like this on a regular basis," Matt chimed in, grabbing another biscuit.

Ry laughed. "That's because you have a bottomless pit for a stomach. Seriously, though, I'm very thankful that we're all able to be here together on this day. I don't know what I'd do without you all."

"We love you too," Matt said. "And now, a toast. To Katie and Samuel, for taking such good care of us and preparing this wonderful meal!" Matt raised his glass but was interrupted by a loud knock at the door. They all froze, barely daring to breathe.

"All right, you two, get upstairs. Samuel and I will take care of this." Katie motioned them out of the room, then she and her husband rose and headed for the door.

The scene was reminiscent of the one several weeks prior, however, this time the officer was in gray rather than blue. Thankful for small blessings, Katie sighed in relief.

"Message for Captain James, ma'am," he said.

Though she hated that Matt might be called out again, she was in constant fear that someone would come after Ry. Her heart was still hammering in her chest, and Samuel, steadfast as ever, reached out and twined his fingers through hers, steadying her as she struggled to regain her normal calm demeanor.

"Just this way, sir," she said, inviting him in. "Would you like a bite to eat? We were just finishing up, if you'd like a plate." She nodded toward the dining room. "I'll go get Matt for you."

"Thank you, ma'am. Food sounds wonderful, if it's not too much trouble." He followed Samuel to the table, as Katie ran up the stairs.

"It's safe. You both can come out. There's a soldier here with a message for you, Matt. I sent him in to get a bite to eat. Might as well get a hot meal while he can."

Matt nodded. "I'll be right down." He turned and looked at Ry. "I want you to stay up here. They may know I have a sister, but it's still probably safer if you're out of sight. Don't want anyone getting ideas once I'm out of here again."

Ry rolled her eyes, but after the last couple of weeks, she knew better than to argue. "I've seen enough trouble to last me for a while," she said. "Besides, I think if I even look at food again, I may throw up."

"Ha! You'll be back down there, eating again in an hour," Matt teased as he walked out of the room.

"Captain!" Standing awkwardly, with a mouth full of ham, the soldier saluted as Matt entered.

He smiled. "Please, don't stand on my account. Eat up. What brings you out this way in the snow?"

Wiping his mouth, the soldier swallowed the last morsel of food then reached into his coat. He pulled out a sealed letter and handed it over. "I'll be ready to ride out whenever you are."

Matt sighed as he broke the seal and quickly skimmed the contents. "Guess I'll get to packing. We'll need to ride hard to get there before they start the attack. I'll see if Katie can wrap up some of this dinner to take with us. No reason for it to go to waste. Finish up. I'll be back in just a few minutes, and we can move out."

He stopped in the kitchen and spoke quietly with Katie for a brief moment before heading up the stairs to deal with Ry. "She's really not going to like this," he mused. Shaking his head, he stepped into her room. She was lying on the bed, dozing. Her fiery hair was already starting to grow back, and it blazed against the stark white of her pillow.

He lightly touched her arm. "Hate to wake you, pretty one, but I'm going to have to leave."

Her eyes flew open. "What? When?"

"Now. They're gearing up for some sort of major action tomorrow near Mine Run. Apparently, they can't live without my awesome battle prowess." He flexed his muscles in jest.

"No, you can't leave." She jumped out of bed and grabbed his arm tightly as a wave of dizziness washed over her.

Matt watched as her face turned as pale as the pillow. "Everything okay?"

"Fine… fine… just got up too fast." She waved him off with a shrug then grinned. "Probably just all that food shifting around in my belly. But you—you can't go. You promised."

"I know what I said, and I almost made it. It is Thanksgiving, after all. I wouldn't go, but they need

207

me. We have a good opportunity, and we need to take advantage of it. Hard to argue with that."

She rolled her eyes at him. "I can argue with it all I want to." Sighing, she hugged him tight. "Just please be careful. I don't want to lose you."

"You won't. I promise." Without another word, he headed to his room to pack up his gear.

Ry was still standing at the edge of her bed when she heard his footsteps on the stairs. Moving to her window, she watched as Samuel brought the horses around. Not being able to hold them back any longer, she let the tears stream down her face as Matt and his fellow soldier mounted up and rode off into the late afternoon shadows. The hoof prints in the newly fallen snow served as a stark reminder of their passing long after they had disappeared from her line of vision.

CHAPTER THIRTEEN

Virginia: November 27, 1863

It was just before midnight when the full implications of what Matt had said hit her.

"Oh my God… Eli!"

She was out of bed in an instant, the vestiges of sleep vanishing as the adrenaline coursed through her body. Grateful for the silvery moonlight that was filtering in through the window, she went digging through her chests, flinging garments out of the way as she searched desperately for the warmest clothes she could find. The snow had frozen over, and the night air was bitterly cold. She was going to need to bundle up well if she didn't want to freeze to death before she reached her destination.

"Lucky for me it's only just past the full moon, so there will be plenty of light." Her mind darted ahead to the upcoming ride. She was still rushing around frantically when she heard the light tap on her door. "Yes? Come in," she said distractedly.

"What in God's name is all this commotion?" Katie looked shocked beyond belief at the chaos Ry was causing in her room.

"Have to go. Have to warn Eli." She kept moving, almost trance-like. After pulling on her old cast-off drawers and shirt, she layered another pair over them then settled on a thick woolen overshirt and pants. She doubled up the socks too then pulled her boots on over them.

"Ry, you need to stop. You know you can't go out there. Besides, Matt will have my hide if I let you go off again." Katie reached out and grabbed Ry's arm. "Look at me!"

"What?" Ry looked up, her eyes unfocused, barely acknowledging that there was anyone else in the room with her.

Katie was nearly frantic with worry. "What is the matter with you?"

"I have to go!" she exploded. Shaking free of Katie's grip, she ran from the room.

"Fool girl. Gonna get yourself killed," Katie whispered, her shoulders sagging in defeat. "Hope he's worth it."

Ry got her horse saddled in record time and was pounding down the road less than an hour after she had awakened. The night was crystal clear, and the moonlight gave everything around her an ethereal glow. The wind chilled her face, and she wrapped her scarf tighter around her head. Her bullet wound was still pulling a bit, but it wasn't anything that she couldn't endure. Cutting across the fields, she could only hope to reach the Union encampment before the battle started.

"I'm not a traitor," she swore to herself. "But I can't let him die."

The hours passed quickly, and she could see the faint edges of the sunrise peeking over the far mountain ridges as she neared her destination. She had run out of the house without much of a plan, but if nothing else, the ride had given her plenty of time to think.

"My plan worked well enough last time, should serve enough for a quick in and out again," she said to herself. "Now if I can just figure out where Eli and his men are camped. Definitely don't want to have to ride through the whole blasted army to find him."

She rode the last few miles in silence, grateful for the warmth of the rising sun on her back. Her fingers, even within the woolen gloves, were nearly frozen, and she wasn't entirely sure if her nose was still attached to her face or not. Exhausted and beginning to despair, she nearly gasped out loud as she came out of the tree line and saw Meade's army spread out before her.

"Dear God!" she whispered in awe.

The encampment where Matt had been held had seemed enormous to her, but this dwarfed it many times over in comparison. She stopped for a few moments, waves of hopelessness washing over her, and it was all she could do not to give up and go back home. Gazing over the fields in front of her, she looked desperately for any sign of the familiar, no matter how small—anything that would put her closer to finding Eli's location within this seething mass of people.

In the end, getting into camp was easy enough. There were plenty of men milling around, so one more didn't seem to rouse anyone's suspicions too much. Still, locating Eli was a daunting task, and if she didn't find him soon, she was going to be stuck in the middle of battle.

"Shouldn't have come here, Ry," she whispered to herself. "This isn't anything like before." Shivering, she kept going, feeling less sure of herself by the moment. She was riding around the eastern flank when her luck finally ran out.

"Well, well… What have we here?"

213

She had been so intent on looking around her, she'd nearly run the man down. Staring at him in surprise, she recognized the bulldog-like guard from the night Matt had escaped. She'd never gotten his name, but it was clear the change in scenery hadn't done much to fix his less than sunny disposition.

"Come back to spy a little more, have you?" he asked, leering at her.

"What? No! I…" Ry was horrified. Visions of her first night in camp sprang up before her eyes, and she wanted nothing more than to turn and flee.

"Get down," he motioned with his rifle, not waiting for her answer.

Willing herself to stay calm, Ry slid slowly from her horse, doing her best to avoid any sudden movements that he might take as an invitation to shoot her on the spot. She needn't have bothered. As soon as her feet hit the ground, he sprang on her, wrenching her arms behind her back and throwing her to her knees.

The cry of pain escaped her lips before she could stop it. "Captain Webb said that I could join you all here if I wanted. Said you could still use the help," she stammered, trying desperately to keep the fear from her voice.

"More like you're looking to do a little more spying… just like before," he said again, ignoring her excuses.

Slinging his rifle over his shoulder, he pulled out a vicious-looking dagger. Ry's eyes went wide with unfeigned terror, and she searched frantically for anyone in the growing crowd who might vouch for her, at least long enough for her to get out of there with her hide still intact. She had almost given up hope when her eyes met Cam's, and she watched the dawning look of horror on his face as he realized what was happening.

"Hold on," he mouthed.

She acknowledged him with an almost imperceptible nod, praying that she had the strength to keep her wits about her long enough for him to fetch

Eli. Then watched as he turned and ran, pushing his way through the mob surrounding her.

True to her promise, Ry was holding on, but just barely. She was curled tightly in a fetal position, having long since given up trying to plead her innocence. In her mind, the only thing that mattered at this point was survival.

"To think I was coming to warn you," she sobbed softly into the cold dirt.

Already, bruises were forming in various places, and blood trickled from the corner of her mouth. Suddenly, the guard yanked her to her knees, his hand gripping her injured shoulder like a vise, and she cried out at the unrelenting pain.

"You know what we do to spies like you, don't you?" He grinned maliciously, running his blade slowly down her cheek. Though it didn't break the skin, the cold steel pressed against Ry's soft flesh, sending her toward the edge of insanity.

She stared at him mutely, eyes wide in abject terror, the fear robbing her of any ability to form coherent speech. Distantly, she could hear others in the mob calling for her death, screaming for the vicious obscenities he could unleash with his knife. With her death so near, the only saving grace was that they'd not yet realized she was a woman. To her last breath, she would be eternally grateful, as long as they didn't find out. As bad as the situation was for her now, if they knew, things would get infinitely worse. The thought was almost more than she could bear.

As she feared the end, thoughts of Matt, of home, and finally of Eli ran through her mind. So much was left undone, left unsaid between them. With no time left for regrets, she closed her eyes tight and prepared for the killing blow.

Cam burst into the officer's tent, nearly knocking the closest guard off his feet. "Oops, sorry 'bout that," he said, trying to catch his breath. The men inside looked up briefly, then turned back to the map they were studying. Catching Eli's attention, Cam motioned for the captain to join him outside then stepped back through the flaps.

"Excuse me, gentlemen," Eli said. "Hopefully, this won't take long." Then he followed Cam out of the tent. "What in God's name—" Eli started.

"We have a serious problem," Cam said, cutting him off with a wave of his hand. "Franklin's got your wife."

It took a moment for the words to sink in, but when they did, Eli's eyes turned to darkened steel. "Where?"

Not waiting a minute longer, Cam took off running again, this time with Eli right on his heels.

When they finally reached Ry, it was all Eli could do not to launch himself directly at Franklin and beat him bloody. He felt Cam's steadying hand on his shoulder and firmly pulled his emotions in check. Unrestrained anger would only serve to get them all killed, and though dying was still a possibility, Eli figured it was worth trying a different approach first.

"Back away from my wife."

Despite his fear and anger, Eli spoke the words calmly, almost conversationally, but they had the desired effect. Whether it was the general respect with which most of his men held him, or simply the fact that anyone had dared stand up to Franklin in the middle of the unfolding chaos, the sudden silence was deafening.

"Your *what*?" Franklin tightened his grip on what little there was of Ry's hair. His knife, so recently pressed against her skin, hovered in the air between them as he finally saw through her disguise.

She whimpered, her body shaking uncontrollably, despite all efforts to keep it still. Looking at Eli, she pleaded silently with him to end her pain.

"Darling." Eli's voice was a husky whisper as he drew closer to the pair. "You should have told me you were coming. I would have sent a better welcoming committee."

He clenched his fists. The urge to kill the man standing in front of him was strong, and he shook with suppressed rage. Cam had his back, as always, and there were other men in the crowd he could count on in a pinch, but it would be much better if they could end this without bloodshed. The mob was riled up, and as bad as it was already, things could get a lot worse in an instant if they weren't careful.

"I'm going to ask nicely one more time… Take your hands off my wife." Without waiting for a reply, he reached out, grabbed Ry's arm, and slowly helped her stand.

Ry's legs threatened to buckle, and she kept an iron-hard grip on Eli, as even the smallest movement sent waves of excruciating pain through her body. It was only through a supreme force of will that she didn't collapse sobbing into his arms.

"This ain't the end of it, Webb," Franklin threatened. His face had turned an ugly shade of red in anger at Eli's interference.

Not bothering to respond, Eli led Ry away from the dispersing crowd. She stumbled once and would have gone down if he hadn't caught her. Then, ignoring her protests, he swept her up into his arms and carried her back to his quarters.

Eli's tent was, all things considered, rather spacious and comfortable. As an added bonus, in preparation for the harsh winter that was coming, it was equipped with its own brick fireplace to help ward off the unrelenting cold that would eventually set in. He stepped quickly through the flap and set Ry down gently on the bed.

"Don't move," he said. Then, stepping back outside for a minute, he motioned to Cam. "Let the majors know I'll be back with them in just a few minutes, please." He ran his hand over his face, and for a brief moment, all the fear he had been holding threatened to overwhelm him. "Jesus, Cam, if you hadn't been there…"

"But I was, and you were… and that's all that matters." He gave Eli's shoulder a squeeze. "Don't be too hard on her, or yourself," he said knowingly. Then he grinned maliciously. "Maybe if we're really lucky, some bastard will put a bullet into Franklin sometime soon."

"Yeah, I could live with that." Eli sighed then turned serious again. "Thank you, Cam."

"Anytime. Now go take care of your woman so you can get back to doing your job before they court-martial you."

He ducked back into the tent and saw that Ry was still sitting exactly where he'd left her. Slightly curled on her side, she was staring into space, her eyes wide with shock. He'd seen men in the aftermath of battle with similar looks, and it scared the hell out of him to see such an expression on her face.

"Ry?" Eli went over to her and knelt in front of the bed. He wanted to yell, scream at her for being such an idiot, but the words died in his throat. "How bad is it, love?" he asked, running his fingers gingerly over the blossoming bruises.

"Hurts all over," she whispered. Her voice was raw from screaming and pleading. Suddenly, she was shaking again, tears streaming down her face.

He drew the blankets up around her and pulled her into his arms. "Shh... it will be okay. I'm here; I won't let anyone else hurt you." Rocking her gently like a baby, he soothed the chills away.

"I'm sorry," she said after the worst of it had passed. The shaking had stopped for the moment, but still, she clung to him, fearing that if he let her go, it would start up again.

"What exactly were you thinking, coming back in here like this?" he asked her finally.

"I don't think I was really." She shook her head. "I... well... you'll laugh." She had the grace to look embarrassed. "I was coming to warn you. I just didn't really realize how big the full army was. It's nothing like before." She spread her arms out vaguely, indicating the incredible mass of tents surrounding them.

"Wait, warn me about what?" he asked, a puzzled look on his face.

"Well, Matt got called back, something about an attack that was being planned, but that doesn't make a whole lot of sense now that I'm here." She noticed the puzzled look on Eli's face and stopped. "What?"

"We're the ones getting ready to attack them, not the other way around." He sighed. "Guess this means that it's not going to be as much of a surprise as we would have liked it to be."

She shook her head. "Guess not."

She went silent again, and for a few moments, he just held her, trailing soft kisses along the curve of her neck. Snuggling closer, she turned her mouth to his. Heat blazed between them, and he deepened the kiss, wanting nothing more than to devour every part of her.

All else momentarily forgotten, Ry shifted then gasped in pain. "Oh God." She flushed in embarrassment.

Eli nipped playfully at her lip then sat back. Standing, he eased Ry carefully to her feet. "Guess we should take a look at you and make sure there aren't any serious injuries."

"I'm fine." Ry hugged her body protectively. "Really." Seemed almost silly to be shy now, but more than anything, she didn't want him to see how battered and broken she was.

He kissed her again then his eyes turned to liquid steel. "I promise you, he will pay dearly for every mark he's put on your precious skin."

She was near to tears again, and she struggled to hold them in, at least until he was gone. Reaching out, she cupped his face in her hands. "I'll be fine. Besides, you need to get back to your men."

She still couldn't really stand on her own, though, and the slightest exertion was proving to be too much for her. Sitting again on the edge of the bed, she willed him to leave so she could bathe the filth off her body without having to endure his pitying gaze.

She could feel the chills coming on and desperately didn't want him to see her break down again.

"I'll get Cam to bring you some extra food and some more water, along with some supplies so that you can clean up. There should be some clean clothes in that chest over there." He pointed to the ornate cedar chest at the foot of the bed. "Don't know that we'll see you much in the next few days." He lifted her chin gently, impressing the importance of his next words upon her. "Do not leave this tent for any reason. I mean it! Please, Ry," he nearly begged. "I can't do what I need to do and worry about you too. If you need anything, there will be a guard right outside, likely either Kent or Bobby. You just tell them, and they'll get it for you. Stay and rest."

She nodded, too tired to argue. She didn't need to tell him that the very thought of going back out there without him terrified her. She stood carefully, ignoring the pain, and wrapped her arms around him, kissing him soundly.

"I love you," she whispered, as he walked out of the tent. It didn't matter if he heard the words or not, it only mattered that she finally acknowledged what her heart had been telling her all along.

She looked longingly at the bed, wanting nothing more than to just drop and sleep. Instead, she limped her way over to the washbasin and slowly started removing her layers of clothing.

Ry nearly jumped out of her skin as Cam ducked in. "Holy Jesus!"

Cam turned, quickly averting his eyes. "Pardon me, ma'am. Just dropping off these for Captain Webb."

Ry blushed, pulling her shirt back across her breasts. "It's fine," she said. "Besides, at this point, I'm fairly sure that my modesty is safe with you."

"You didn't show those to Eli did you?" He nodded at the bruises that covered nearly every inch of her body.

"God no… and don't you go telling him either. I'm sure he'll see them later, but for now, he needs to be able to focus on keeping you all alive. He can deal with me later, assuming you crazy fools don't get yourselves killed in the next couple of days." She kept her tone lighthearted, but Cam—astute as ever—saw right through her brave facade.

"Anything I can do to help?"

She shook her head, more grateful than he would ever know for his care and concern. "Don't think anything's broken, but I'm gonna be sore for a while." She grinned. "For once, I think I'm going to listen to my elders and rest."

"Sounds like a good plan to me," he said seriously, ignoring the jab. "Take care of yourself, you hear?"

"You too, Cam… and thank you."

He nodded and headed back out, leaving Ry to bathe her wounds in peace.

It took longer than it should have, considering she'd had to re-stitch her chest. The rough treatment had ripped the old stitches clean out, shredding her newly healing skin. By the time she was done, it was all she could do to stand, the muscles in her legs long since past the point of exhaustion. Not even bothering to rummage through the chest, she wrapped the blankets around herself and slept like the dead.

CHAPTER FOURTEEN

Virginia: November 28 — December 1, 1863

The days that followed were some of the longest Ry had ever experienced in her life. Rescuing her brother had been bad enough, but the constant shelling and ground-shaking madness that was going on around her was likely to drive her insane if it didn't end soon. Worse than anything else was not knowing if Eli or her brother were still alive, or if they were among the hundreds of dead that littered the battlefield. When Eli had said there wouldn't be word, he'd meant it. He had apparently stopped back by long enough to grab his gear, but she'd been sleeping. The only evidence he had been there at all was the letter she now clutched in her hands.

She had not even noticed it immediately. It had taken three days before she'd even had the energy to do more than get up to relieve herself then lie back down. The pain had been so intense that any other movement had left her shaking and near tears. That first morning after she'd woken up, she had moved most of the basic rations within arm's reach of the bed, so at the very least, if she was hungry, she would not have to go far. Otherwise, she would have likely starved. Only when the pain had finally started to subside, had she been bored enough to start rummaging through the tent, looking for some sort of distraction. That was when she'd found the letter.

No flowery protestations of love or impossible-to-keep promises that he would return unscathed from battle. It simply read...

Last Will and Testament

of

Elijah Grayson Webb

In the event of my death, I bequeath all my earthly possessions and any future monies due to me, to my wife—Rylee James Webb.

She wanted to tear it up into little bits and scatter it to the winds. She knew why he had done it, of course. But she couldn't bear it if he was dead. Managing a measure of control, she folded up the letter and sat it back on the desk. Feeling slightly nauseated again, she curled up on the bed and nibbled at a stale biscuit. She debated making soup, but the thought of moving made her stomach heave, so she settled back and watched the candlelight dance with the shadows.

The fourth day dawned clear and cold. The sounds of battle seemed more distant, and Ry fervently hoped that meant it would all be over soon. She got up and gingerly made her way around the tent, working cautiously to get her strength back. She had not made it more than a few steps before the waves of dizziness hit her, and it was all she could do to stumble to the chamber pot before she started vomiting.

"God, Ry, what the hell is wrong with you?" She splashed cool water from the basin over her pale face. Holding on to the furniture, she made her way to the chair near the entrance of the tent. Tying back the flap, she sat down, hoping the fresh air would chase away whatever bug was plaguing her. She was still there, asleep and half frozen, when Cam found her. The late afternoon sun setting low in the sky.

"Are you crazy, girl? You'll catch your death sitting here."

"Mmm... what?" she murmured sleepily. "Oh... guess I must have dozed off. Still not been feeling very well, and everything I do just takes it out of me. Eli with you?"

"Not yet. Should be back soon, though—tonight or in the morning by the latest. Sent me back up here to check on you. Hate to admit it, but your boys seem to have kicked our arses good this go around." His normally happy demeanor seemed subdued, and she noted the exhaustion in his eyes.

"If you need to sleep for a bit, please feel free. There's an extra blanket in the chest if you want to grab it for me. I'm really quite comfortable here in this chair."

Cam brought her the blanket and sat it on the edge of the chair. "Eli loves that chair. Found it just sitting in the field, not too far from here one day when we were out scouting. Guess some people are lucky like that." Without another word, he stretched out on the bed and fell asleep instantly.

"Sweet dreams," she whispered.

Closing the tent flap, she rummaged around for a bite to eat then settled back in the chair to wait for Eli.

CHAPTER FIFTEEN

Virginia: December 2, 1863

It was over.

Oh, there were still a few dumb bastards shooting at each other, but at this point, the majority of the killing was well over and done with. Shivering violently in the pre-dawn chill, Eli sincerely considered just dropping to the ground where he stood. But he was pretty sure that if he did, he would never get up again. He wasn't injured, or at least he was fairly certain that he wasn't. It was somewhat hard to tell, considering the amount of blood and muck he was spattered with. Still, he was bone-weary, and if it wasn't for Ry waiting back at camp for him, he would have simply given up on the spot.

The sun was barely a smudge on the horizon as he eyed his horse, which was lazily standing just a few short paces away. "Evil beast," Eli growled. He was only a step or two away at best, but it might as well have been miles in the shape he was in.

With a groan, he dragged himself over, grabbing at the reins that were nearly out of reach. He started to hoist himself up then stopped as his horse nudged him. Looking down, he barely saw the bloody leg peeking out of the brush in front of him.

"Just another poor gray bastard that didn't make it," he whispered sadly to the horse.

"Fuck you, Webb!"

The feeble reply had Eli turning sharply, back on alert, pistol in hand. Slowly, he moved closer and sighed, lowering his gun. "Jesus, Matt, you have the worst of luck, don't you?" He might have laughed, but he didn't think the man on the ground would find it nearly as amusing as he did.

"If you think I'm going back to rot in some dilapidated prison again, you can just kiss my hairy white arse," Matt replied.

"Was my company that bad?" Eli asked mockingly. "Seriously, though, how bad are you hurt?"

"I'd like to say just my pride, but I do believe that I'll be sitting out the rest of the war with this one. Hell, I'll be lucky not to lose my leg unless someone can get this stupid bullet out." He grimaced as he tried to sit up, but the pain proved too much for him, and he collapsed back into the dirt, panting from the exertion.

"Okay, here's the deal." Eli lowered himself down carefully so that Matt could hear him clearly. "I'm going to get that ugly-arse jacket off of you, seeing as how you won't be needing it again anyways, then we're going to load you up on my horse. Might just be that I've got someone who can patch you up."

"Why would you want to do that?" Matt asked warily.

"What? Can't I just do an old friend a favor? You wound me to the quick." Eli gave him an injured look then, not waiting for a reply, grabbed his arms. "Ready?"

237

"No, not really. But don't guess you're giving me much of a choice, are you?"

"Well, there's always another choice," he said soberly. "In this case, your other choice is to lie there and die, I suppose. But I assure you, your sister would kill me." Eli sighed then continued. "Despite it all, I find I'm rather fond of life, so if it's all the same to you—"

"What about my sister?" Matt's tone was icy as he interrupted, and Eli shifted uncomfortably under his penetrating gaze.

"Look, let's get you up and moving, and I'll explain as best I can along the way. Longer we sit here, better chance some fool with an itchy trigger finger is going to come along and take a shot at us."

Matt bit off a scream as Eli lifted him off the ground.

"You scream like a girl," he teased. It might have seemed cruel, but Eli was truly afraid that Matt would pass out on him. So he kept up the jibes, needling him almost mercilessly until he was safely on

238

the horse. "Warn me if you think you're going to fall off. I really don't want to have to lift your sorry arse up off the ground again." Eli took hold of the reins.

"If I fall off a horse, it will be because I'm already dead. So you can just leave me if it's too much of an inconvenience for you. Now start talking!"

They moved cautiously over the field. Eli casually looked around for a spare horse he could commandeer without drawing too much attention to the two of them. It was going to be very slow going if he had to walk all the way back to camp.

"Talk!" Matt said again, not letting up.

"Pushy one, aren't you?" Eli replied, then he turned serious. "I hope you do understand about last time. If I had been there when you were initially captured, maybe it would have been different, but as it was, my hands were pretty well tied."

"War is hell; I get that." Matt shrugged. "I want to know what is going on with you and my sister."

Eli kept his face averted, and in truth, he felt like a little kid caught with his hands in the cookie jar.

Worse, it was more than just a little mortifying to find that he wanted Matt's approval. Not that he had all that much say at this point, but Eli still wasn't sure that Matt wouldn't stick a knife in his gut once he explained the situation. And it was damn clear that Ry hadn't bothered to say anything either, even though she'd had ample time to do so.

"What exactly did Ry tell you?" Eli asked finally.

"Not much," Matt replied. "I rescued her just south of Culpeper when you were on your way up here to camp. At the time, she only mentioned that she had been injured on her way home, and that you patched her up."

"Ahh… I wondered what happened. Thought she just up and left me."

"What do you mean up and left *YOU*?" Matt asked pointedly.

"Well, guess you should have been just a little bit quicker in your rescuing." Eli let out a sound halfway between a laugh and a sob. The sheer

240

absurdity of the whole situation had him very near to cracking.

"What's that supposed to mean? What did you do to her?" Matt nearly launched himself from the saddle despite his injured leg, only prevented from doing so at the last minute, as Eli held him in place. In Matt's weakened condition, he was no match for Eli, and after a few moments, he quit struggling.

"Didn't do anything to her. Only wanted to keep her safe," he whispered, his voice soft with emotion. "She's my wife."

Matt just stared at him with the slack-jawed look of someone who had just been poleaxed. He had no idea exactly what he thought was coming, but whatever possibilities had been kicking around in his mind, that surely wasn't one of them.

"You know, if I was whole, I'd run you through right now," he said finally, fingering the dagger still strapped to his belt.

"Yeah... figured you would," Eli replied soberly. "If it makes you feel any better, I promise to still be around when you are, and if you feel the same way then, you're welcome to have a go at me."

They walked on in silence, carefully avoiding the dead that littered the field. They passed a number of troops from both sides, but all were busy caring for the injured or helping to bury the dead. In any case, none gave Eli or Matt much more than a passing glance as they went by. Several times, Matt opened his mouth to say something, only to shut it, leaving the words unspoken.

Nerves stretched taut until Eli finally exploded. "With all these damn bodies, you'd think there'd be at least one loose horse. Not that I'm an uncaring bastard and all, but I don't have two days to walk through all this mess."

Matt looked at him and burst out laughing, clutching at his side when the pain became too much to handle. "Really, of all the things, that's what you complain about?" He tried to get himself under control.

"Don't see why you think it's so funny," Eli growled. "It's your lazy arse that's hogging my horse."

"Well, maybe your eyesight is just failing you in your old age." Matt needled him, payback for his earlier taunts. "There's one right over there." He motioned to their left.

"Oh, thank God!" Eli nearly cried in relief as he mounted up.

Despite Matt's seeming alertness, Eli was truly worried about him. Already, he could see the fever burning in Matt's eyes. They needed to get to Ry, and quick. Stepping up the pace, they raced across the field toward camp.

Ry heard the horses coming and roused herself from the chair, thankful that the worst of yesterday's dizziness seemed to have passed. She was on her way to check on Cam, when Eli burst into the tent with Matt over his shoulder. He dropped her brother carefully into the recently vacated chair and walked over to where Cam was still sleeping.

He kicked the end of the bed with his boot. "Rise and shine, lazy bones."

"I'm up. I'm up," Cam murmured sleepily.

Having heard that one a million times before from her brother, Ry was impressed to see that—fully awake or not—Cam was actually up and standing at attention, ready for whatever Eli needed him to do.

"Need you to see if you can get a medical kit and a bottle of whiskey if you can. At the very least, some bandages and the booze."

"Be right back," Cam said, already on his way out of the tent.

"What's wrong with him?" Ry asked, terrified by the heat she felt coming off of her brother in waves.

"Shot in the leg. Probably be fine once you get the bullet out and clean the wound, but it took us a while to get here, so the infection is already setting in."

Ry cleared off Eli's desk then walked to the basin and washed her hands. "Let's move him up here.

I'll need light as well. Get as many candles as you can, so I can see what I'm doing."

She was back in professional mode, afraid that if she didn't keep her mind focused strictly on the task ahead of her, she would break into a million pieces. Cam had said Eli was fine but knowing and seeing were two different things. She wanted nothing more than to fall into his arms and shower him with kisses. But her brother's life was hanging in the balance, so for now, everything else would just have to wait.

Cam walked back into the tent and grinned. "Jackpot! Not only got a full kit and a bottle of the major's finest, but brought some supper as well."

"Thank you," Eli said, handing Ry the supplies.

She turned to Matt, thankful that he was still unconscious for the moment. "Eli, can I borrow your knife, please?" She reached out as he handed it to her.

Deftly, she slit Matt's pant leg, noting with relief that the bullet was lodged in the fleshy part of his thigh. Setting the knife aside, she grabbed the scalpel. She passed it through the nearest candle flame for a brief moment, cooled it in the air, then poured a bit of whiskey over it.

"Hold him down," she said. "And put something between his teeth if you got anything handy; don't want him to bite off his tongue."

Eli eased a thickly rolled cloth between Matt's teeth, then grabbed his shoulders. Cam leaned across his good leg, and carefully held the one Ry was working on.

"Ok… here goes." Taking a breath to steady herself, she cut into the skin. Matt lurched up, screamed once, then passed back out. "Keep him steady!"

Her hands were shaking as she pulled back the flap of skin. Digging her fingers into the muscled flesh of his thigh, she felt around until she touched the hardened fragment lodged inside. Grasping it gently, she pulled with a slow and steady pressure, desperately fearful of breaking it up. Even the smallest bit left in his leg could fester, and he could lose his leg. Or worse, it could kill him if they weren't careful. Finally, it popped free with a gruesome sucking sound, and Ry sagged against the desk, willing her legs to continue holding her upright.

"Almost there, love," Eli said encouragingly.

Cam nodded. "Don't know about you all, but I'm going to need a long pull from that bottle when we're done here."

"Think I may just have to join you," Ry said, giving him a lopsided grin. Turning back to her brother, she sobered. "Looks like Matt's getting the first swig, though." She grabbed the bottle and poured a liberal dose of the alcohol into the open wound. Satisfied that there were no remaining fragments, she sewed it carefully then wrapped the clean bandages tightly around his leg. She looked up. "Well, that's all we can do for now. Just have to see how it looks in the morning."

Eli just managed to catch her as she fell. Whatever fire had been keeping her going through her brother's surgery had winked out, and she had nothing left to give herself when the exhaustion set in.

"Guess I better go see if I can find a few more blankets," Cam said, rousing himself. Though he'd slept clear through the previous night and half the day, it wasn't nearly enough to penetrate the never-ending fog of weariness they had all been living with the last few days. "Think we could all use a good night's sleep, or at least as much as we can get surrounded by all this chaos."

Eli nodded and carried Ry over to the bed, tucking the covers up around her. "What the hell am I going to do with you?" he whispered, not for the first time. He smoothed her hair back from her face and gently kissed her lips.

"Get her outta here as fast as you can, if you know what's good for both of you," Cam said from behind him, tossing Eli one of the extra blankets.

"Mmm," he agreed, continuing to stroke Ry's hair lightly, as he rested on the floor next to her. Her hair was such a beautiful color. He wondered how he hadn't noticed it before. Shaking his head, he turned back to Cam.

"Assuming Matt wakes up in the morning, I'm going to tie him to his horse if I have to and send them both home. She may not like it much, but if they stay here any longer, some bastard like Franklin will come nosing around, and then we're all done for. I'm already skirting the edges of treason as it is, but I'd rather not have to shoot my way out of my own army if I can help it." He would have laughed, but it was a bit too close to the truth for comfort.

Cam nodded, stretching out in the chair. "Well, hope you're comfy there. I'm stealing your chair for the night." He grinned lazily.

"Go right ahead. I'm going to sleep here with my wife." Now he did laugh. "My God... a wife... I really am crazy, aren't I?"

The only answer he received was Cam's snores from across the room.

CHAPTER SIXTEEN

Virginia: December 3, 1863

Ry slowly opened her eyes and found Eli still sitting on the floor, half-hunched over the side of the bed, the heavy weight of his arm across her body. She smiled and twined her fingers with his, relishing the warmth of his skin against hers. Her mind was a bit clouded with sleep, and for a moment, she couldn't quite remember how she had ended up in bed. She moved carefully, not wanting to disturb Eli, and suddenly it all came rushing back to her.

Forgetting her previous caution, she bolted from the bed. "Where's Matt?"

Eli was up in a flash, pistol in hand. "What?" He looked around warily, trying to determine if they were under attack or not.

Cam was up too, and despite it all, Ry burst out laughing. "Oh God, I'm so sorry. I didn't mean to startle you all."

"That's okay, ma'am," Cam said in his most serious tone. "Gotta have someone to keep us on our toes."

"Crazy woman," Eli said, kissing her soundly.

"Enough of that." She shooed him away as the blush rose to her cheeks.

Cam grinned. "Don't stop on my account."

"Men!" Ry threw her hands up and stalked back to Matt's pallet.

It was a convincing performance, but Eli saw the ghost of a smile playing on her lips, and chuckled.

She knelt down beside her brother, and he stirred as she checked his bandages. His skin was cool to the touch with no hint of any noxious odors or the previous day's heat, which might indicate an infection. She was happy that whatever fever had been lurking when Eli had brought him in yesterday evening seemed to be gone.

"Hello there," she said, as Matt opened his eyes. "Nice to see you back amongst the living."

He moved gingerly as he sat up. "Was it really that close?"

"No, not really, but it still gave me quite a scare to see you like that." She ruffled his hair. Already, it had grown back over the patch the doctors had shaved off several weeks ago when he'd first been injured. She had always been envious, for it seemed such a shame for a man's hair to grow so perfectly, when all they did was cut it right back off again.

"You'll likely be sore for a while, and it goes without saying, of course, that you shouldn't be putting any weight on your leg anytime soon if you can help it. The bullet was deep in the muscle, and I had to do a fair amount of cutting and digging around to get it all out. But you should heal up clean, and God willing, it shouldn't keep you from having near perfect use of it in the future."

He squeezed her hand. "Thank you, Ry. Don't know what I'd do without you."

She nodded, trying to keep the tears from her eyes. God knew this war was turning her into a weepy sap. "Eli's got an extra pair of pants you can borrow." Turning, she motioned to Eli and Cam. "Guessing he's going to need a bit of help if you all don't mind." Ry moved back toward the front of the tent to give Matt some privacy.

"Yes, ma'am!" they answered in unison.

"How you really feeling?" asked Eli, as he and Cam helped Matt to his feet.

"Like hell," Matt said, wincing as he tried to put weight on his injured leg.

"Figured as much." Eli shook his head. "Makes what I have to say next that much worse too, especially given that Ry said she doesn't want you using that thing. But the truth is, I'm gonna have to kick you all out of here."

Matt's expression darkened. "Why bother even having Ry patch me up?" His voice rose, and Ry glanced over at them.

"Keep it down and listen." Eli held his hand out, cautioning Matt to silence. "You can't stay here;

it's not safe… for either of you." He looked back at Ry. "Otherwise, you would be more than welcome."

"It was bad enough that we didn't bother to formally check in last night when we got back to camp," Cam chimed in. "I mean, I ran a bit of interference for us, telling the major that Eli was helping with some of the injured men, but that will only keep them satisfied for so long. If we keep hiding out in here much longer, someone is bound to notice, especially if we have to keep bringing in extra supplies."

"Right now, it's still fairly disorganized out there," Eli said. "The battle might be over, but they'll be picking up bodies and tending to the injured, which makes it the best time to move you all—before someone starts counting heads… if you know what I mean."

Matt nodded. "Can't fault your logic, I guess." Sighing, he leaned heavily on the desk, already dreading the long miles ahead of him. "Now the real question—have you told her yet?" He pointed back at Ry, grinning maliciously at Eli.

Cam laughed. "Think maybe I'll stay out of that one. Might as well have someone left to pick up the pieces that are left over when she's done with you."

"Well, if that's how you're going to be about it," Eli said primly. Giving them both a look of mock dejection, he went bravely to face his fate.

Ry just stared at him, her mouth a perfect little O of shock. "You want me to leave you? Now?" she finally stammered.

Eli sighed. "It's too dangerous here, and you know it. Cam and I were desperately hoping someone would shoot Franklin, but I saw the damn bastard out there earlier, and he's just itching for a reason to call me out over you. He's still not convinced that you aren't a spy, which under present circumstances, I might be a bit hard-pressed to prove otherwise." He nodded back at Matt.

She understood immediately and quieted as he continued. "I don't want you to go, but if you stay, I don't know that I can keep you safe. And it will only get worse once winter really sets in. While we relish the downtime, the boys get bored. They'll be looking for something to keep them occupied on those long winter nights, and you've already seen how some of them like to play."

Ry shuddered at the memory he evoked—not only of her own beating, the marks of which were still emblazoned on her body, but the young Confederate officer she had treated a few weeks back.

"You've made your point," she finally acknowledged. "When do you want us to go?"

"Honestly"—he pulled her into his arms—"just as soon as I can saddle up the horses."

He kissed her softly, savoring the sweet taste of her lips. She pulled him in deeper, and his senses exploded as he lost himself briefly to the madness.

256

They jerked apart suddenly as Cam cleared his throat behind them.

"Pardon me," he said, eyeing them pointedly. "Seeing as you were a bit busy, I took the liberty of bringing the horses around."

"Um… yes… thank you," Eli replied sheepishly, the faint blush visible just above the top of his collar.

"No need to thank me. It's only right that a man should give his wife a proper send off." Cam couldn't keep his laughter in any longer, and his shoulders shook with the poor attempt at hiding his mirth.

Eli swatted at Cam. "Bugger off!"

Looking back at Ry, he turned serious and cupped her face gently. "When you get home, stay there—no matter what… please."

Taking his hand, she nodded, her face grave.

Eli savored her touch. "I don't know what else this war has in store for us, but I need to know that you're safe, or it will likely drive me to distraction.

Men who are distracted make mistakes, and mistakes kill."

"Stop." She held a finger to his lips as visions of his body, cold and dead, swam before her eyes. "You don't need to say anything else. I promise. Just come home to me safe." She threw her arms around him as hot tears fell down her cheeks.

He held on to her for dear life. "I'll do my best."

Eli and Cam helped Matt mount up.

"I'm thinking that it might be best if Ry rides behind you for a while, just to help keep you steady," Eli said. "You'll have two horses, so you can switch off if you need to, but really, your best bet will be to ride straight through."

Noting the sheen of sweat on Matt's brow just from what little energy he'd expended, Ry nodded in agreement, her eyes full of concern. "The quicker we can get home, the better it will be. As it is, I'm worried the ride is going to split his stitches."

"There's extra bandages in the saddle bag if you need them," Cam said, patting the worn leather satchel.

"Thank you." She pulled herself up behind Matt and placed her hands lightly on his waist.

"Cam and I will lead you around to the outer edge of camp. Just follow along and let us do the talking if anyone stops us."

Ry and Matt both wore civilian dress, and they'd burned the ragged remains of his gray uniform earlier. He had hated to do it, but if they were caught anywhere near the Union army with it in their possession, they would both be hanged for sure—especially once they left Eli's company.

"Let's head out." Eli nudged his horse, and they rode slowly through the camp.

Most of the other soldiers were busy and paid no attention to them, but every so often, there were those that took notice as they passed. Ry could feel their hate-filled gazes, and soon, her nerves were stretched tight.

"Just keep going," Eli whispered, pulling up next to her. "Nothing to worry about." But the glance he exchanged with Cam spoke volumes.

Matt wasn't oblivious either, and though he kept his body relaxed, his training kicked in, and he was on alert for any possible sign of attack. It came soon enough.

"Sneaking out like the traitorous scum you are, I see."

Ry tightened her grip on Matt as Franklin moved into sight. They had just reached the last row of tents, and it was clear he had been waiting for them. No doubt he'd been warned they were coming by one or more of his cronies they'd passed along the way.

A few of them were still hovering nearby like a pack of rabid dogs, mindless and drooling, sniffing for the scent of blood that was sure to spill. Eli and Cam had been hoping that someone would have put a bullet in Franklin during the previous days' battle, but no such luck. He had come out the other side nearly unscathed.

"That's the second time you've made disparaging remarks about my wife," Eli said, his tone deadly. "Considering how lucky you were that I didn't kill you for your actions the first time around, I'm honestly surprised that you're putting yourself in for round two. Really thought you were smarter than that; guess I should have known that you weren't." He hadn't reached for his gun yet, but his muscles were quivering in anticipation of action.

"Fuck you, Webb!" Franklin sneered, echoing the same sentiment Matt had expressed in jest only the day before. Yet in this case, the epithet was dripping with months of repressed anger and hatred.

Eli slid down from his horse. "That's Captain Webb to you." Keeping his eyes on the danger in front of him, he motioned for Cam to keep Ry and Matt moving. His mission was the vital one, and at this point, Eli would do what he could to give them enough time to get away safely.

Despite her fears about having to face Franklin again, Ry started to protest. "No! We need—"

But Cam cut her off with a terse shake of his head. Leaning in close, he whispered, "Let him handle it. It's been a long time coming, really, even before you came around. Needs to be taken care of, and there's no time like the present."

Ry hesitated, torn between the need to get to safety and the desire to keep the man she loved from harm, but then she recalled Eli's last words to her and gave in. Not wanting to be a distraction, she nodded reluctantly and followed Cam into the trees. It was a hard lesson to be sure, but if she couldn't obey him now, how could he trust that she would keep her promise in the future?

Though he itched to watch them leave, Eli kept his eyes trained on Franklin. Still, he listened intently until the sounds of the horses faded behind him, then he breathed a long sigh of relief. *Now, if she doesn't come racing back here, we'll have really made some progress.* He resisted the urge to grin at the thought.

Franklin was thrown by the smile that slid briefly across Eli's face. "What's so damn funny?" he demanded, angry that he had been unable to stop Ry from leaving. Once he had understood that she was a woman, he'd had fevered dreams of pounding her bloody, in more ways than one, and being denied was almost more than he could take.

In a rage, Franklin motioned for some of his boys to follow the riders, but the amused look vanished from Eli's face in an instant and he shook his head. "Don't even think about it," he threatened. And just like the dogs he'd compared them to earlier, Franklin's pack recognized the menace in Eli's tone and shied back like the cowards they truly were.

Turning back to Franklin, he lost the battle to control his temper. Closing the distance between the two of them, he grabbed the front of Franklin's coat and slammed him to the frozen ground. Eli relished with childlike glee the loud smacking sound of the man's head bouncing off the cold, hard-packed dirt. "This is between you and me, you sorry son of a bitch."

Needless to say, the situation went downhill from there. In the normal course of things, Franklin was no real match for his captain. Eli might have been older by a number of years, but having attended West Point, he was wiser and more experienced at gauging an opponent. The men were of nearly equal height, and though Franklin weighed a good forty pounds more, most of it was flab from the years of debauchery he'd been living before the war. The hard riding they had been doing over the last year or so had done little to change that, but now Franklin's pent-up anger drove his already vicious temper to new heights, and he channeled his hate into every punch.

He considered the emotion of love useless and weak. Having never understood it, Franklin underestimated the lengths to which a man would go in order to protect the woman he loved. Where other men would have long since curled up and died—or at least wished they were dead—from the ferocity of Franklin's blows, Eli shrugged them off as if they were nothing. The cut above his left eye was giving him a bit of trouble, as the blood flowing freely from the wound was beginning to obscure his vision. But on the whole, he seemed unaffected by the brutal damage being inflicted on his body.

Not that Eli wasn't landing a few choice punches of his own, but even though they were effective, they were still few and far between as he continued to let Franklin spend his fury more or less unchecked. Though painful to endure, as a distraction it was working well, giving Ry and Matt the extra time they needed to get safely away. And in the end, Eli's seemingly casual treatment of the encounter was slowly driving Franklin insane.

"Why won't you go down?" Franklin's face was livid, with mottled shades of red and pale white, and the veins in his temple were standing out in stark relief against his skin. The exertions were finally taking their toll. He was nearly incoherent, his chest heaving as he gasped for air.

It was the opportunity that Eli had been waiting for, and he smiled maliciously through the pain, savoring his victory. For his part, Franklin never even saw it coming. Distracted by his inability to take his opponent down, Eli slid under his guard. Fueled by his own pain and unrelenting rage at the horrors this man had unleashed—not only on Ry, but on countless others over the last few months—he delivered a stinging uppercut that sent Franklin crashing to the ground, his eyes rolling up into the back of his head. Taking advantage of their reversed positions, he pinned the barely conscious man to the ground and continued to pummel him. Eli landed blow after vicious blow, until he heard the sharp crack of Franklin's nose breaking and felt the hot blood splash over him.

His fury only somewhat abated, a small part of Eli's mind recognized that if he didn't stop, he was like to beat the man to death with his bare hands. It was a sobering thought, not that Franklin didn't more than deserve it, but Eli wasn't looking to spend the rest of his life in prison, or worse—hanging from a rope over such a sorry piece of refuse. Fighting for control of himself, he stumbled back to his feet, barely managing to maintain his footing as his body rebelled against the pain. Breathing hard, he watched warily for any sign that the bastard was going to get back up again.

"Don't think you need to worry too much about that," Cam said congenially from behind him, causing Eli to nearly jump out of his skin.

"Jesus, Cam, don't do that do me."

Eli leaned heavily on his lieutenant. Now that the fight was over, the pain was almost overwhelming, and he fought the darkness that hovered at the edge of his vision.

"They get out okay?" he asked.

"Of course." Cam looked a bit hurt. "Did you think I would do any less?"

"No… no." Eli shook his head, wincing. "Still, had to ask, or you might think I didn't care." He tried for a grin, but his split lip put a stop to it almost immediately.

"How much trouble do you think I'll be in when we get back?" Eli asked, nodding at Franklin's inert body. He still wasn't sure that sticking a knife in the bastard's gut wasn't the better course of action. If he thought he had any chance of getting away with it, he would have, just to be on the safe side. Though, to be sure, Eli was fairly certain that having beaten Franklin within an inch of his life in full view of his pack mates, it was unlikely that any of them would be causing too much trouble in the future.

"Not much, I'd imagine," Cam said seriously. "You put the fear of God into his little buddies. Hell, they took off running before ole Franklin's body even hit the ground." He grinned at the memory of the craven little dogs running for their lives. "I'd be surprised if they so much as breathe in your direction anytime soon, much less report this to anyone. Like as not, they'll all be model soldiers for the rest of this godforsaken war."

"We can only hope." Eli sighed, kicking Franklin's boot. "Guess we should drag his arse back to the infirmary."

"Dunno." Cam shrugged. "He seems awfully comfortable where he is. If his friends don't even want to help him, don't see why we should bother, either. Besides, with any luck, he'll freeze, and we'll be rid of him once and for all."

"Eh… not like I can lift him in my condition, anyways," Eli agreed, holding a hand to his bruised ribs. "And he'd certainly not do the same for me if I was the one lying there."

"Mmm." Cam nodded. "Ain't that the truth."

Limping over to where his horse was standing, Eli bit back a cry of pain as he mounted up. "I'm going to be lucky if I can even stand tomorrow," he said, groaning. Then without another word, he and Cam turned and rode back into camp.

CHAPTER SEVENTEEN

Virginia: December 4—7, 1863

The trip home very nearly killed Matt.

They had to hide from patrols twice, one Union and one Confederate, and each time they dismounted, his wound ripped open a little more. He was losing copious amounts of blood, despite the additional bandages, and Ry was beginning to despair long before they reached the tree-lined drive that led to their door. It was well after midnight when she finally saw the lone light shining in the distance.

"Bless Katie for always leaving a candle lit." Nearly weeping with relief, she prayed desperately. "Just a bit further; we're almost there."

He had lost consciousness not long after the last patrol, and it was taking the last bit of Ry's strength to keep him upright in the saddle. Wrapping her arms tightly around him, she urged her mount forward into a gallop. Throwing caution to the wind, she raced the last mile to the house, afraid in her heart that she had already wasted too much time in getting them home.

Katie heard them coming. She had always been a light sleeper, even more so since the war had started. She heard the hoof beats pounding hard on the dirt road, the sound carrying loudly in the still night. Ry saw additional points of light appear as other candles were lit, and she was eternally grateful to see both Katie and Samuel on the porch when she rode up.

"Help me get him down," she begged, sliding off the horse. Her legs buckled as they hit the ground, and she grasped the saddle for support to keep from falling.

"Miss Ry, come on now," Katie said, helping her into the house.

Samuel followed, the big man holding Matt gently in his arms like a baby. Matt would have been mortified if he'd known, and any other time, Ry would have laughed to see it. But for now, it was all she could do not to cry.

271

"God, please don't let him be dead!" she prayed, racing up the stairs to get fresh medical supplies as they put Matt in the parlor, lying him across the ornately carved Victorian sofa her father had bought just before his death. Katie had a basin of warm water ready for her when she returned, and she washed up as Samuel cut away the fabric surrounding Matt's wound.

"Hang in there," she told herself, trying to hold back the exhaustion that threatened to overwhelm her. Her whole body was starting to shake, and she felt Katie reach out and place a steadying hand on her arm. Grateful for the support, Ry turned to her task, the simple touch helping to revive her.

Treating the wound wasn't nearly as difficult as it had been before, but the loss of blood was worrisome. Matt was very pale, and the jagged edges of the wound looked red and angry. Wiping away the blood, she washed out the wound again and carefully stitched it closed.

"I could really go the rest of my life perfectly content if I never have to do this again," she said, tying off the last stitch. The little row was neat and tidy, and she noted—somewhat hysterically—that if nothing else, her sewing skills had improved immensely in the last few weeks.

She wrapped the clean bandages around his leg then covered him with the blankets that Samuel had brought down for her. Though a fire was blazing in the grate, she wanted to make doubly sure that he didn't catch a chill while he slept.

"It bothers me that he didn't even stir through any of that," she said with frown. Sitting briefly on the edge of the sofa, she ran her hand gently over his hair, watching him for any sign of movement. When none came, she sighed, her shoulders slumping.

"Nothing more you can do right now, Miss Ry," Katie said. "Why don't you go get some sleep. You're near to dead on your feet as it is."

Ry started to argue, but the look Katie gave her was more than enough to silence her. Though she wanted nothing more than to crawl under her blankets and sleep for a week, she also couldn't leave her brother when his life was hanging in the balance.

"Tell you what," she said, attempting to placate Katie. "I'm going to curl up here in this chair with a mountain of blankets. That way, if Matt wakes, I'll be close enough that I can check on him. But I can still get some sleep, so you don't have to worry about me. I promise I'll call if I need anything."

"Mmm… see that you do," Katie said, eyeing her closely. Then she and Samuel headed back to their room to get some much-needed rest.

Ry was dreaming, tossing in the chair and murmuring frantic sounds of protest in her sleep. Franklin was beating her again, his heavy fists battering her already broken body as she curled desperately into a protective ball on the cold and unyielding ground. Moaning in pain, she surfaced from the darkness, her eyes staring blankly. Shaking herself free from the spell, she glanced around the room, breathing a sigh of relief as she recognized the parlor.

"Home," she murmured, snuggling deeper into her blanket. Its warm comfort chased away the remainder of the nightmare.

The moaning continued. Confused at first, Ry listened intently, and when it came again, it finally dawned on her what she was hearing. Jumping to her feet, she raced to Matt's side. Heart in her throat, she watched in horror as he thrashed around on the sofa. He was soaked with sweat, and she reached over to untangle the blankets wrapped around him. She laid a soothing hand on his brow to calm him and quickly snatched it away again. His hot skin was almost painful to the touch.

"No!" she cried, fear coursing through her.

She could feel the heat coming off of him in waves, the fever ravaging his already weakened body. "Katie," she shouted, running to the kitchen.

The following days blended together into one long haze of exhaustion. Sponging his body, they would get him cooled down, only to have the fever shoot back up again as soon as they stopped. Ry had removed his bandages the first day, checking the wound desperately for any sign of infection, but it was pink and clean just as it should be, and the skin was already starting to heal.

"I just don't understand it," she sobbed helplessly on the third day.

Katie ran a hand over her hair, trying to soothe her as best she could. "Sometimes, there's just nothing to be done." Her eyes were filled with sorrow. She had raised them from infancy, helped them bury their mother and their father. In her heart, Ry knew that losing Matt on top of it all would nearly kill them both.

"Let's try sitting him in the tub for a while." Ry was willing to try almost anything at this point to quell the raging heat that was consuming Matt from the inside. "Maybe if we immerse his whole body, it will make a difference."

Katie nodded. "Can't hurt to try. I'll get Samuel to bring the tub in, and I'll fetch some more water."

Ry sank into the chair, barely able to hold herself up. The dizziness was back, but seeing as she couldn't even remember the last time she had eaten anything, much less slept, it wasn't surprising. She only meant to close her eyes for a moment but was sound asleep before she even noticed. She was startled awake when Samuel brought in the tub and quickly rose to help him fill it.

"You need to sleep, Miss Rylee," he said.

"Can't." She shook her head. "Not until his fever breaks for good."

"Well, when we get him outta the tub, you're going to sleep for at least a few hours." He held up his hand, silencing her protests. "Don't argue! What good are you to anyone if you make yourself sick?"

Samuel was a man of such few words under normal circumstances that when he finally did speak, others generally listened closely to what he had to say.

In any case, he didn't wait for an answer as he moved to Matt's side and gently began removing his soiled clothing. It was something that should have been done a lot sooner, but between the exhaustion and the fever, Ry had just never gotten to it.

Samuel tossed Matt's blood-spattered pants to the floor. "Think maybe I'll just burn these."

"Mmm," Ry agreed, as she moved to the foot of the sofa. She helped Samuel lift Matt from the couch and stumbled a bit as they eased him into the tub. He was shaking all over, drifting in and out of consciousness. At times, he shouted incoherently, jumbled words that just tumbled forth without rhyme or reason. At other times, he rambled, talking to their father about day-to-day chores, or sometimes even replaying conversations he'd had with their mother. He dredged up memories from so far back that Ry was truly scared he meant to go off and join them both. Heartsick, she could only watch, unshed tears shining bright in her eyes.

"You hurt, Miss Ry?" Katie asked as she brought a stack of clean linen towels into the room.

"What? No," she said, confusion plainly written on her face.

Katie motioned to her. "There's blood on your hand."

Ry looked down, staring at her red-stained fingers. "Well, I..." She turned back to Matt and motioned for Samuel to ease him back up just a bit from the edge of the tub.

The wound on Matt's back was such a tiny thing, not much bigger than the tip of her little finger, but it was red and angry. It had scabbed over, but she must have caught the edge of it when she had sponged his back. Exposed, the blackened wound was oozing foul liquid.

"Oh God!" she breathed. "I should have looked." Wringing her hands, she continued to berate herself.

"There, there." Katie's voice was like a balm to Ry's soul. "You did the best you could. We'll take care of it now, and he'll come 'round. You'll see."

"I hope so." She still worried that they had found the source much too late to save his life.

They moved Matt back out of the water, dried him, and wrapped him in clean blankets. Samuel sat beside him on the sofa, supporting his body, as Ry worked on cleaning up the wound.

"That something so small could be so deadly..." She carefully cut away the infection. Nicked by someone or something in the heat of battle, like as not, Matt had never even felt it. He certainly hadn't noticed the injury when he'd been coherent afterward. The pain in his leg had overshadowed anything else.

When Ry had finished bandaging it up, she sighed. Though it was likely just wishful thinking on her part, Matt already seemed to be resting easier, and though the fever was still hovering, he did seem to be just a bit cooler than before.

"All right, Miss Rylee"—Samuel laid Matt carefully back on the sofa—"go get some sleep." She started to protest again, but the look he gave her brooked no arguments. "Don't you worry; I will be right here. Promise I won't move an inch. If you're needed for anything, I will send Katie right up to wake you."

"Thank you," she said simply, stumbling out of the parlor.

In her room, she removed her dress. The effort to do so was almost too much for her. She had changed once, on that second morning. Having looked down at herself in moment of disgust, she'd practically ripped the soiled clothing she'd been wearing from her body. Since then, they had been so busy, it had been the least of her worries, but she was grateful now to be shedding the offending garment. Like it or not, she'd need to burn her dress too. She knew it would be useless to even try to remove the blood and sweat stains that were splattered across it.

Desperately wishing for a bath, she settled for a quick sponging off. Then she threw a warm flannel gown over her head and crawled into bed. Sinking into the softness, she pulled the blankets up tight around her, willing away all the aches and pains that racked her poor body.

"God, please let Matt be okay," she prayed. "I can't lose anyone else." Unable to hold off sleep any longer, she closed her eyes and dreamed of the day when the war would be over and they all could be happy again.

CHAPTER EIGHTEEN

Virginia: December 8—24, 1863

Ry slept through the night, and sunlight was pouring into her room when she woke. For the first time in days, she felt rested. She had forgotten to bank the fire in the grate before she'd gone to bed, though, and the air in her room was downright chilly. Dreading the cold, she snuggled deeper into the blankets and briefly considered just pulling them up over her head and going back to sleep. Her belly rumbled, and she sighed, sliding out from under the covers.

"Guess being lazy isn't on the menu this morning. Besides, need to check on Matt," she mused. Samuel or Katie would have called her if he'd gotten worse in the night, but that didn't stop her from feeling guilty for not being by his side.

The chickadees were chirping outside her window, and she stopped to watch them hop on the sill. It was a beautiful cloudless day, and despite the cold, she stared wistfully, wishing Matt was well enough to go outside and enjoy it with her. Dressing quickly in a long brown woolen day dress to ward off the chill, she made her way down the stairs and into the parlor. There was a tray on the table, and the scent of warm coffee nearly made her swoon. She poured a cup and savored the rich flavor, its warmth invading her body.

"Good morning, Miss Rylee." Katie put a plate of eggs and ham into her hands. "Sit and eat. Matt's been resting comfortably all night. He can wait a few more minutes for you to get more than a morsel or two of food in you."

"Yes, ma'am." She nodded, sniffing gratefully at the mouthwatering smells emanating from the plate. "Thank you for looking after him for me."

"It's what I've always done, ain't it?" She smiled, her voice warm with affection. "Been lookin' after the two of you since you were born. Certainly not going to stop now."

Ry set the plate down and hugged her tight, "And we'd have been lost without you."

Katie grinned, patting her cheek. "Don't I know it."

"You two gonna keep at your bawling, or can't a man get any sleep around here?"

Ry turned sharply, and with a cry of joyous relief, ran to Matt's side. "Hush, you!" she said, laying a hand on his head.

His pale skin was cool to the touch, and the eyes that regarded her, though sunken deep in his face, showed no signs of the fever that had raged so virulently for the last few days.

"You gave us such a scare," she said.

He grinned. "I'm not that easy to get rid of."

Still, he needed Ry's help to sit up, gasping with the effort. Once she had him positioned properly, she propped him up with some pillows, and Katie brought him a bowl of hearty broth.

"You keep that down well enough, we'll see about getting you something a bit more substantial," Katie said, as he gazed mournfully at the liquid. "Don't want you to make yourself sick."

"Yes, ma'am," he said grudgingly, echoing Ry's earlier words.

Ry sat next to him on the couch and picked at her own plate, sneaking him a bite or two when Katie wasn't looking. She gauged to a tee the moment when his strength ran out, and his eyes began to droop again.

"Think you can make it up the stairs to your bed, or you just want to stay down here and nap for a while longer?" she asked, taking the bowl from him and setting it on the table.

The rhythmic snores from his side of the sofa were his only reply.

"Guess that answers that." She grinned, covering him back up with the blanket. Picking up their dishes, she carried the tray back to the kitchen and helped Katie clean up.

The blazing warmth of the fire soon had her dozing as she sat at the table, and finally, Katie shooed her back to her room. "Might as well get as much rest as you can," she said. "Once he really starts coming 'round, he's going to drive us all crazy."

"God help us all!" Ry laughed as she wandered off to her room.

From then on, Matt made steady progress, and as Katie predicted, the days of forced inactivity as his wounds slowly healed were hard on them all. If it had just been the injuries themselves, Matt might not have been so bad, but the fever had taken a lot out of him, and he spent most of the first few days weak as a newborn kitten. Ry and Katie were his constant shadows, ready to grab his cup or help him stand when the effort of holding it, or himself up, proved simply too much for him to handle. For a man like Matt, needing such help was humiliating.

"You are being such a baby," Ry finally shouted at him. She had only left him for a few moments, and though it was foolhardy, he'd tried to stand up on his own.

He glared back at her petulantly. "I wanted to sit by the window."

"Stubborn fool!" she countered, helping to lift him off the floor where he had fallen. "You should have said something. That's the whole point of me asking, *'is there anything you need?'* before I walk out of the room."

"I shouldn't have to ask. I'm a grown man."

Defeated, he teetered awkwardly then plopped back down on the sofa, wincing as the stitches in his leg pulled tight at the sudden movement. "I'm sorry, okay? I just hate being confined and having to rely on you to do everything but wipe my arse."

"Tsk... tsk... such language." She laughed, kissing the top of his head. "Still, I know it's hard, but if you overdo it, it will take that much longer for you to recover. So be a nice boy and stop fighting it."

He grinned, flinging a rude gesture as she turned to go. "Bugger off!"

"Hrmph!" Trying her best to look offended, she stalked out of the room.

As soon as he'd woken from his bout with the fever, Matt had sent word to his commanding officer, advising his superior of his condition. The army had sent around one of their own doctors to check him over, and in the end, the doctor had agreed with Ry's assessment of his recovery. To their relief, word had come a week later, in the form of another gray-clad messenger, that he was being discharged from the Confederate Army.

Captain James,

We greatly appreciate the high level of service you have given. Due to the nature of your injuries, you are hereby honorably discharged.

Sincerely...

He read the words out loud as he skimmed over the letter. He was already determined not to go back.

Treason or not, he was more than done with being shot at, but it was nice to have it officially in writing.

"At least now I won't have to skip town," he said, refolding the letter. "Though I'm still not convinced that some nice little village out West isn't the best place to be these days."

"But Matt, this is your home." Ry was appalled that he would even consider leaving.

"I know, but honestly, even if this war ends, I don't think it's ever going to be the same here. There's just too much…" He stopped, but she could see the horror of the last couple of years reflected in his eyes. "I… I just don't know any more."

She nodded and put her arms around him, resting her head on his shoulder. "Still, I don't know what I would do if you weren't here with me." He'd been her rock since the day she was born—"*a sacred duty*"—he'd told her once. Laid on him by their father on the very day of her birth, though he'd never treated her as just an obligation.

"Well, you can always come with me. We could start fresh, ride the open ranges. It would be a great adventure!"

"You're really serious about this, aren't you?" she asked, a note of concern in her voice.

She could see the excitement in his eyes and wondered how she could have missed it. They'd talked often as children about traveling, and of course, he had gone off to West Point. But with the war, those dreams—at least for her—had long since been put up on the shelf, forgotten, never even to be dusted off on rare occasions.

For a brief shining moment, she imagined what traveling would be like. No cares in the world; just riding off into the sunset, camping under the stars. The peacefulness of not having to see anyone else in the world if they didn't want to, and most of all, visiting the pristine lands untouched by the war and hate that marred her home state. She wanted it desperately, and part of her really wanted to say yes, but she shook her head, watching the light in Matt's eyes darken as she shook her head.

"You know I can't," she said softly. "Eli told me to wait here, and I promised him that I would."

"You really love him?" Matt asked her.

She nodded without a hint of hesitation. "I do."

"Do you think he loves you?"

"Dunno. I mean he has to care, at least somewhat. Why else marry me? Or risk his life for me—or you for that matter. You've known him longer. Would he do that for just anyone?" She was bordering on hysteria, all the fears and uncertainties welling up inside her, ready to go off like Katie's old tea kettle.

At a loss as to how to comfort her, Matt instantly regretted even asking her such a thing, and he thought carefully before he answered.

"I liked him well enough, at least when he wasn't on the other side of the field from me. He's also honorable and loyal to those who are close to him, so I think he will take his vows seriously." He reached out to hold her hand. "But I don't know what that means in terms of you. Would he have married you just to keep you out of trouble? Yes, I think he would have. Does that mean you still can't build a future together? I just don't know."

He watched the emotions slide across her face. Despair and sadness slowly turned to determination and fragile hope.

A fierce new light shone in her emerald eyes. "Well, I don't know either, but I have to stay and find out. If it turns out that he doesn't really want me, that's just his loss, isn't it?"

"That's my girl!" Matt said with a grin, hoping in his heart that it would all work out for her in the end.

The next few days were a flurry of activity. Christmas was coming, and since they were going to all be together for the first time in several years, they were going all out. With Matt supervising, the house was soon full of fragrant evergreen boughs and colorful ribbons, and there was a definite festive feeling in the air. Having been down for so long, it was nice to see a bit of lightheartedness back in their lives, even if it was only for a brief, shining moment.

Katie and Ry went over the household stores meticulously, planning for the feast. "It might not be much, but we're together, and that is what really matters," Ry said as she rolled out the dough for a pie crust. Once it was good and flat, she set it into the pan. Then she sat down, resting her head in her hands.

"You okay, Miss Rylee?" Katie asked.

"Fine… fine. Just tired."

In truth, her fatigue was starting to worry her. She had been sleeping regularly now that Matt was on the mend, and while the bone-weary exhaustion was gone, she was still plagued by a distinct lack of energy. She'd also started to notice the pronounced dark circles under her eyes.

"You need to eat more." Katie shook her head, her eyes filled with concern. "I've seen how you just pick at your food when you think I'm not watching."

"I try, honestly I do, but it just doesn't seem to sit well with me these days." She laid a hand on her belly. "God, hope I'm not coming down with something."

Katie stared at her for a moment then burst out laughing. The sound echoed off the kitchen walls.

"What's so funny?" Ry asked, eyeing her suspiciously.

"Oh, I'd say you're coming down with something, all right." Katie rolled her eyes. "Psh, and you're supposed to be a doctor." Cackling, she went back to stirring the pot of stew.

"What's that supposed to—? Oh… Oh!" Ry's eyes flew wide open as it hit her. "Can't be… can it?"

"Well, seeing as you didn't even bother to invite me to the wedding, don't know that I should even talk to you about it," Katie said primly.

She was only teasing, but Ry knew they had both dreamed of the day Ry would walk down the aisle—a perfect wedding for her precious girl. Of course, the one she'd had less than fit those sweet childhood dreams, but nothing could be done about that now.

"It wasn't like that, and you know it," Ry said soothingly. "Besides, it was only... well"—she blushed furiously—"just the one time. Guess I didn't even think about it. So much else going on." She cupped her belly lovingly. "Huh... a baby. This just might be the best Christmas present ever." With her eyes sparkling and a wild grin on her face, she hugged Katie tight. "I love you!"

The letter came for her on Christmas Eve. The sight of a Union boy on the porch had given them all a fright, but once it was clear that he was just there to deliver the message, things settled back down. To

Matt's chagrin, Ry even invited him in for a bit of holiday cheer, to which the boy thankfully declined.

"Have a few other places to get to before the day is out," he said. "This was a bit out of my way, but I owed Captain Webb a favor. Sorry it took so long for me to get it to you."

"Thank you for bringing it." Ry was full of gratitude, sending him off with extra foodstuffs to eat or share with the others when he returned.

"When you see Captain Webb again, tell him I've been keeping my promise."

"Yes, ma'am." He nodded then remounted and rode back out into the winter chill.

"Well?" Matt asked when they returned to the parlor.

Ry looked at him pointedly. "Well what?"

He nodded at the letter in her hands. "What's it say?"

She ran her fingers over the dust-stained paper. "Haven't opened it yet, have I?"

Eli's handwriting fit his personality, bold and strong. No hesitation or poorly formed letters. This was a man comfortable with his thoughts, knowing just how to express them to others.

When Ry looked up, everyone was still staring at her.

"What?" she demanded. "Can't I just enjoy having it for a moment?"

"Of course, dear," Katie said. "Don't mind us at all. Matt, why don't you come help me in the kitchen for a moment?"

"But I just sat down," he complained.

"Now Matthew," she said, pointing toward the door.

"Fine, I'm going." Walking from the room, he stuck his tongue out at the back of Ry's head.

She laughed. "I saw that."

In the silence that remained, she savored the letter for a few moments longer. Holding it up to her nose, she could almost smell Eli's scent and could imagine him sitting at his desk, writing the words.

"God, I miss him," she whispered, slowly pulling the tattered pages from the envelope. Skimming over the contents, she felt her heart drop like a stone.

Dearest Ry,

Don't have a lot of time but wanted to let you know that I'm being sent out of the area. Don't know how long it will be before I'm back this way, or if I'll ever be. Praying that this war ends soon, so that we can all have a normal life together. Stay safe.

Eli

It was dated the morning after they'd left, but knowing how things were these days, it wasn't surprising that it had taken this long to reach her.

"Guess I should be happy they delivered it at all," she mused.

She sat there, clutching the letter in her hands, just staring at the fire in the grate and trying to reconcile the fact that it might be years before she saw her husband again. Not that he had said he would be able to visit, or that she even had any expectation that he would. Still, the idea of him being nearby had been a comfort. Now he was gone, and she didn't even know where. She also didn't know when or if he would be back, or even how to contact him if she wanted to. All she could do was pray that whatever happened, he would return home safely to her in the end. Unable to contain them any longer, Ry let the tears roll silently down her cheeks, staining the paper in her hands.

"Ry, you all right?" Matt asked softly from the doorway.

"I guess." Her voice was thick with emotion. "I mean, everything is fine; no one is dead or anything. Just... he's been moved out; didn't say where."

"Probably couldn't say, Ry. You know how it is," Matt said comfortingly. "He doesn't know I'm out, not to mention something could have happened to his messenger. He's just limited in what he can say, you know?"

She nodded, still staring blankly. "I understand, but it doesn't mean that I like it." She sighed. "Never even got to tell him about the baby."

"Baby? What baby?" Matt exclaimed, his eyes going wide with shock.

CHAPTER NINETEEN

Virginia to Tennessee: December 4—15, 1863

"So much for rest," Eli murmured, looking at the message in disbelief.

His body, still battered and sore from the brutal punishment inflicted on him during his fight with Franklin, rebelled at the very idea of getting on a horse, much less going for a 375-mile hell ride through frozen countryside and snowcapped mountains.

He exploded finally, waving the note in Cam's face as he stormed around the tent. "They've lost their bloody fucking minds!"

"What are your orders, sir?"

Though he felt nearly the same as Eli about the insane nature of their newest mission, Cam's tone was all business, and more than anything else, it helped to settle Eli's frayed nerves.

"Gather up whomever is left of the men, at least the ones that aren't too injured to stand. Tell 'em to pack their gear and saddle up. We'll meet here in front of my tent in an hour. Make sure you tell 'em to dress warm. We've got a hell of a long way to go, and no time to stop and smell the roses along the way."

"Yes, sir!" Cam replied as he ran out of the tent.

He would have said they were truly in hell, except that hell was supposed to be blazing hot and full of fire, both of which he would have more than welcomed with open arms at this point. The current conditions were anything but. "Frigid" would have been putting it mildly; even "freezing" didn't quite cover it. At night, the temperature dropped to well below zero, and it wasn't much warmer during the day. They pushed the horses as much as they dared, but despite it all, Eli still wasn't entirely sure the lot of them weren't destined to die somewhere on this godforsaken mountainside. The winds howled through the passes as they climbed into the higher elevations, and even the tiniest bit of exposed skin was at risk.

"This is madness," he said, not for the first time since they'd left.

"Of course it is," Cam agreed, trying to keep his tone as level as possible, given the circumstances. "Can't even imagine what sort of help they think we'll be when we get there... if we get there."

"Oh, we'll get there." Eli gritted his teeth. "But I'm not entirely sure that we won't just fall over when we do. None of us have slept more than a few hours a night, and the horses are nearly blown."

He could feel his men's anger, not that he could blame them. They all should be cozied up by a nice warm fire, bedded down for the winter. "No sane man should be out in this mess." He crouched lower on his horse and pulled the scarves tighter around his exposed face as the day's first flakes of snow began to fall.

The fact that they had made it to Bean's Station in time for the coming battle was due entirely to Eli's

304

stubborn perseverance. Even Cam's normal ability to make the best of everything had wavered as they made the long trek from Virginia to Tennessee. They'd lost two men along the way, one the second night out, and the other just the night before. They had lain down to sleep and simply hadn't woken up again, the brutal cold claiming its due. Unfortunately, the frozen ground had been much too hard to even attempt a proper burial for either of them, so they'd been forced to build cairns. Losing precious time, they had searched for stones that would protect the bodies from any predators that might come in search of an easy winter meal.

Both deaths weighed heavily on Eli, and as they rode on, he sank further into the depression that had been hovering over him for the last couple of days. His thoughts had turned as cold and black as the night around them. Falling in battle, he could understand, but dying like that was just—

"It's not your fault," Cam said, interrupting his thoughts.

Eli stared ahead for a long time before answering. "I know, but it doesn't make it any easier. These are my men, and this is a fool's errand. Hell, there's not even enough of us to make a difference. So why are we here?" Anger flashed in his eyes.

Cam shook his head. "Wish I had an answer for you. Really, I do." Nearing their destination, they hunkered down in their saddles and called for the men to pick up their pace.

"Let's get this over with, so we can get the hell out of here."

It was a short but bloody battle, with several hundred men killed on both sides. They may have made it in time to help reinforce the men already picketed in town, but as Eli had known all along, it wasn't nearly enough to make any sort of difference. After two days of fighting, they had beaten a hasty retreat along with the rest of the forces who had been valiantly attempting to hold the town against the enemy. In the end, though, when all was said and done, Bean's Station was in Confederate hands again.

"Now what?" Cam asked, once they were safely entrenched and out of any immediate danger of being attacked again.

"Guess we stay low and try to get some rest. No way we can make it back over the mountains as long as the weather stays like this. And honestly, at this point, I don't think the horses would make it if we tried. As much as I want to be back in Virginia, it's not worth risking anyone's life to get there."

Eli looked disgustedly at the snow that was falling. Already, it was piling up in thick, wet blankets, and as heavily as it was coming down, they would all likely be buried in it by morning.

"Well, in any case, no one is going anywhere anytime soon, so we might as well make ourselves comfortable." He added another log on the fire to ward off the bone-chilling cold. "Hope Ry's having a better time of it than we are," he mused, staring into the flames.

"Seeing as she has an actual roof over her head, I'd say that she's at least one up on us." Cam grinned, his unflappable nature slowly reasserting itself. "God willing, we'll both get back to Virginia soon enough to find out."

"God willing, indeed." Eli nodded, as he curled up under his blanket to get some sleep, praying desperately they weren't still sitting there come spring.

CHAPTER TWENTY

Virginia: August 7, 1864

Matt had been there before, and the memory was unnerving to say the least. Still, he waited in the room where they had left him, pacing back and forth.

"Stay here, out of the way," they'd said. "Don't worry; shouldn't take too long."

That had been hours ago, and to twenty-eight-year-old Matthew James, it still seemed an eternity. His belly rumbled, a not-so-subtle reminder that he had eaten the lunch and the extra treats they had left him much too long ago. He was well-aware these days of what "soon" really meant, but his nervousness had made him hungry, and he had eaten the food all up, for lack of anything better to do.

In the heat of the summer, Ry's pregnancy had made her irritable. Her belly had grown heavier with each passing day, turning her normal graceful movements into awkward clumsiness. But when the labor pains had set in, she and Katie had rushed around in a flurry of activity, shooing Matt off to wait and pace. So he was left alone with his memories of a time long before, when another woman had given birth to a precious babe. He prayed desperately that this time, things would go much differently for all of them.

The door opened. Turning, Matt watched Katie enter the room and set a tiny bundle gently into the cradle. She motioned for Matt to join her, and they looked down at the squalling baby. She was just a little thing, not much to look at—all red-faced and wrinkly—but man, could she holler.

Katie reached over and laid a hand on the polished cherrywood frame then gently rocked the cradle. Her lined face was tired, but her sparkling brown eyes were full of joy, her heart near bursting with happiness as she gazed down at his newborn niece.

Taking a deep breath, she looked up at Matt. "Ry needs her rest, but if you like, you can go in and see her for just a bit."

Smiling, he hugged her as his eyes filled with tears. "Thank you!"

She patted his arm fondly. "Your parents would be so proud," she said, gazing again at Ry's precious little girl.

Matt tapped softly on the door.

"Come in," Ry said, her sleepy voice barely above a whisper.

"She's beautiful," he said, his voice full of pride as he walked into the room.

Ry's face lit up, the exhaustion momentarily vanishing under the radiant glow of her smile. "She is, isn't she?"

"Have you decided what to name her?"

She sat back, lost in thought for a moment. "I've been thinking. I'd like to call her Emily if that's all right with you?" She looked slightly apprehensive.

He sat carefully beside her on the bed. "Why wouldn't it be?"

"It's just, I never knew her... not like you did. I didn't want to hurt—"

"Ry, it's perfect!" he said, cutting off her words with a gesture. Tears shone bright in his eyes, and he wasn't sure his heart could contain such happiness. "You may not have known her, but as you said, I did... well, at least as well as any child could have. But what I do know is this—Ma would have loved that you were naming your daughter after her. Really, she'd be thrilled."

"Thank you." She smiled, her eyes closing as the exhaustion took over.

He kissed the top of her head and let himself out of the room as she drifted off to sleep.

CHAPTER TWENTY-ONE

Virginia: August 7, 1865

The war was over.

It had officially ended back in May, but the last few holdouts hadn't laid down their weapons until the middle of June. Still, there was no sign of Eli. Ry was trying desperately to hold out hope, but deep in her heart, she despaired that he was dead. Matt could hear her crying late in the night when she thought no one would notice.

He'd held off on his plans to go West. At first, he had stayed because he still needed time to fully heal, and then because Ry needed him to help with Emily. She was such a miracle, and her very presence made their lives that much brighter. To Ry's chagrin, he had already been taking her out riding.

"Pa did the same with you," he'd said when she protested vehemently the first time he mounted up with the baby in his arms. Emmy had been barely eight months old at the time and going through a cranky spell. She'd been inconsolable, and they had all been at their wits' end trying to find a way to soothe her, when Matt had taken off with her around the yard. She had quieted immediately, tears turning to laughter, as he cantered with her held securely in his embrace. Her little fist grasped the horse's mane instinctively; it was love at first sight. From that point on, riding was her favorite activity.

"You've gone and spoiled her," Ry said fondly, watching them from the porch.

He grinned as they circled past. "Ahh... but it's so much fun."

The sedate mare was his birthday gift to his niece, and the horse was a beauty. Her pale coat glistened in the warm August sunlight. He had spent a good bit of the summer fashioning a harness of sorts, one that would allow little Emmy to ride by herself as he or Ry led her around the yard. He'd run nearly the length of the county trying to find the perfect horse, one that wasn't too spry or headstrong. When he'd found Moonlight, he'd known instantly that she was the one.

It helped too, that her previous owner had a lovely daughter of his own, which was the final reason Matt was still there rather than riding the ranges out West. They were waiting even now for Miss Josephine and her father to arrive for Emmy's birthday celebration. Though it was early August and the height of summer, the day was still fairly comfortable. Hot as usual, but a breeze was blowing in from the east, carrying a hint of the rain that would surely be coming within the next day or so. Matt swung Emmy down from the mare and walked with her up the front porch stairs.

"I'll take her in and clean her up," he said, as Ry eyed her dust-covered daughter.

"Good idea," she said with a grin. "I'll be there in just a moment."

Still, she sat, staring out across the fields. "Eli, where are you?" she asked softly, her heart near to breaking again. She had been so sure he would be home in time to see his little girl turn one, but there'd been no sign, no word. She'd heard nothing at all since the letter he'd sent nearly two years before when he had been sent off to God knew where in the middle of winter.

"Did you even make it to where you were going?" She wiped at the tears threatening to fall. "Not today. You promised yourself not to do this today," she admonished, but she didn't move, only closed her eyes and prayed to whatever God was listening for a miracle.

She heard the hoof beats long before she saw the rider. As she watched the lone figure draw closer, she wondered briefly if Josephine had ridden ahead of her father. "Leave it to Matt to find a woman who loves to ride almost as much as he does." She smiled, happy that her brother had someone in his life that would help him move on from the horrors of the last few years.

She frowned. "That doesn't look like Jo, though." Standing, she brushed out her skirts and walked down the steps to meet the incoming rider.

Eli pulled to a stop just short of her and awkwardly dismounted. Grasping the pommel of his saddle for support, he pulled a stout walking stick from the sheath tied to his horse.

"Oh!" Ry cried. Her heart hammered in her chest, barely daring to believe what her eyes were showing her.

"Hello, Ry," he said almost shyly.

He was much leaner than she remembered, and his hair had a touch of silver that definitely hadn't been there before. He limped toward her, leaning heavily on the walking stick.

Without any hint of hesitation, Ry launched herself at him, taking care at the last moment not to knock them both to the ground. His mouth crushed hers in a blaze of need, and she lost herself in the sensation. Drawing back finally, she stared up at him, reaching out to trace the deeply etched lines in his face. Those were new too, along with the haunted look in his sea-blue eyes. A look that only hinted at the hell he had endured since they had last parted.

She kissed him again. "I'm still here," she said. "Just like I promised."

"I'm very glad to see that," he said softly, his voice hoarse with emotion. He had been keeping it bottled up inside for so long, and now that he was safe within her arms, it was as though a dam had burst. Everything came pouring out.

"Come… sit with me." She wrapped her arm through his and led him onto the porch. They sat on the bench she'd so recently vacated, holding hands, and for several moments, they simply reveled in each other's presence.

"I'm so sorry," he finally said.

"Shhh…" she said soothingly. "It's all right. You're here now, and that's the only thing that really matters."

He shook his head, searching for the right words. "For so long, they didn't even know if I was going to make it." He stopped, swallowing hard. "Even once I was on the mend physically, I was still half out of my mind for quite a bit longer." She squeezed his hand, offering comfort and encouragement. "Got caught up in the Fall of Petersburg. Mortar round exploded right on top of us. I still don't know why I'm here... Everyone else..." He stopped again, tears streaming down his face, his voice shaking uncontrollably.

"Everyone else... just gone. Killed instantly, or so they say. Cam was standing right in front of me, and it's probably what saved my life." He was sobbing now, the grief too painful to bear. "I remember the blood, then nothing until I woke up in the hospital."

Ry put her arms fully around him, holding him and willing him to let go of the guilt and pain he was carrying around with him.

"It's not your fault," she said, her heart breaking. It broke not only for Eli, but for Cam, who had been one of a kind. She could still see his smiling face and would forever admire the sunny disposition he'd exhibited, even in the face of madness.

"By the time I realized that no one had notified you, I knew it would be just as easy for me to come and tell you myself. Cam would have normally handled that sort of thing, but…" He trailed off, not bothering to state the obvious.

"I'm so sorry, love," she said.

He rested his head on her shoulder, and for a while, they just held on to each other, mourning the loss of a close friend.

"Hey, Ry." The door opened, and Matt poked his head out. "You coming? Oh!" He took in the scene with a glance. "Welcome home, Eli." He felt truly happy to see the man he had once thought to run through for deigning to even mention his sister's name. "Just in time too, I see. Ry was beginning to think you weren't going to make it."

"In time for what?" Eli asked, confusion written clearly across his face.

Matt looked at Ry. "You didn't tell him?"

"Well, we have a lot of catching up to do," she said evasively. Turning serious again, she held her brother's gaze. "Cam's dead. Thought you'd want to know."

Matt's eyes darkened, and he reached out a comforting hand to Eli. "Real sorry to hear that. He was a good man."

Eli nodded, his grief showing plainly for all to see. "One of the best."

"Well, I hate to interrupt, Ry, but you're needed inside," he finally said, once he'd gotten his emotions back under control. "*Someone,* who should have been napping, somehow managed to crawl into the kitchen and dump a pan of cake flour on herself," he whispered cryptically.

"Oh, for crying out loud!" she exclaimed. "How does one small child manage to constantly defeat four grown adults?" Exasperated, she stood up and headed into the house.

Eli stared after her. "You up and get married while I've been gone?" he asked Matt. "Congratulations!"

"Um... well... not..." Matt just sputtered. "Actually, there's the light of my life right now," he said, saved from answering as Jo and her father came cantering down the lane. "We're not married yet, but I'm definitely thinking of popping the question soon."

Eli was at a complete loss, and Matt wasn't looking to enlighten him. Once he made quick introductions, Matt motioned to Eli. "Why don't you head inside? Trust me, it will be fine." Grinning, he watched his brother-in-law walk into the house.

"Surprise!" he whispered.

Ry was in the kitchen with Katie, cleaning up one hell of a disaster. The *someone* was seated on the floor, banging a small pot with a wooden spoon, and she looked curiously at Eli as he entered the room.

Looking down at her, he smiled. "That's an impressive mess for one so small."

She giggled and reached her arms up to him. Ry's breath caught in her chest, and she grabbed Katie's arm.

Without hesitation, Eli swung Emily up into the air and settled her on his hip, bracing himself against the counter for extra support. "Aren't you a precious one?" He tweaked her nose with the tip of his finger. Suddenly, his blue eyes went wide, and he looked up at Ry.

She saw the question in his face and moved toward them. "Eli, this is Emmy." Putting her arms around both of them, she said, "Emmy, this is your papa."

Emmy looked up at her papa, for the first time putting a face to the word her mama had been so meticulously teaching her in the short time she had been learning to talk. Her blue eyes mirrored Eli's in miniature perfection, and she gazed lovingly up at him, reaching out a tiny hand to his cheek.

"Papa!"

The answering grin on his face was priceless, and he kissed Ry, even as he snuggled his daughter closer.

"Welcome home, love!" Ry said, kissing him back.

THE END

Made in the USA
Coppell, TX
03 July 2022

79534461R00194